ELLIOT STANTON

Pawnbroken - The Scripts

Copyright © 2022 by Elliot Stanton

All rights reserved. No part of this publication may be reproduced, stored or transmitted in any form or by any means, electronic, mechanical, photocopying, recording, scanning, or otherwise without written permission from the publisher. It is illegal to copy this book, post it to a website, or distribute it by any other means without permission.

This novel is entirely a work of fiction. The names, characters and incidents portrayed in it are the work of the author's imagination. Any resemblance to actual persons, living or dead, events or localities is entirely coincidental.

Elliot Stanton asserts the moral right to be identified as the author of this work.

Designations used by companies to distinguish their products are often claimed as trademarks. All brand names and product names used in this book and on its cover are trade names, service marks, trademarks and registered trademarks of their respective owners. The publishers and the book are not associated with any product or vendor mentioned in this book. None of the companies referenced within the book have endorsed the book.

First edition

This book was professionally typeset on Reedsy.
Find out more at reedsy.com

Contents

Pawnbroken - Series Synopsis	1
Pawnbroken - Episode Synopsis	3
Pawnbroken - Character Biographies	9
Episode 1 - My Girl	12
Episode 2 - Mad World	56
Episode 3 - Electric Dreams	97
Episode 4 - Hot In The City	143
Episode 5 - Party Fears Two	189
Episode 6 - True Colours	237
Episode 7 - Lonely This Christmas	286
Contact Elliot Stanton	343

Pawnbroken - Series Synopsis

Pawnbroken is a half-hour situation comedy set in a pawnbroker's shop named *Trueman's* in suburban Greater London. It is essentially Jim's story. He co-owns and runs the business alongside two assistants, Patrick, who has been with him since leaving school and from the second episode NATALIE. The other original second assistant, Carl, tells Jim at the beginning of the first episode that he is leaving. A replacement has to be found, and Natalie is hired.

A constant thorn in Jim's side is his ex-wife and co-owner of the business, Vanessa. She doesn't work in the shop but is anything but a silent partner. She knows she can typically get her ex-husband to do (and pay for) anything she asks, but sometimes oversteps the mark, and he hits back but never lands a knock-out blow. They share one daughter, Lucy, who is a daddy's girl.

Each episode is typically set over the business day and is almost exclusively set in the shop premises. The action at work is bookended with Jim's car journey to and from work and is accented with his thoughts, both spoken out loud and narrated in voice-over. Each individual scene begins with a shot of or an audible clue to the time, whether it is a wall clock, watch, radio announcement, car clock, Town Hall clock chimes, etc. The title of each episode is one of Jim's favourite songs and will give a clue to the story's theme.

Due to the shop environment, the three main characters (Jim, Patrick and Natalie) enjoy a camaraderie, making Vanessa envious. Other regular characters include George, the self-important window cleaner and Mrs Mullaney, the ditzy, curry-making octogenarian who regularly cooks barely edible food for the staff.

Another one of the main themes is the relationship between Natalie and her older ex-boyfriend, Kit. (whom we don't meet until the final episode) and his ever more extravagant gifts he sends Natalie to win her back.

We will see many other customers who aren't recurring characters.

As the series plays out, it becomes more and more evident that Natalie will reconcile with her ex, but just when Jim believes that he has no chance with her at all, fate steps in and offers a helping hand. This incident has the side benefit of causing great upheaval in the life of his nemesis, Vanessa.

I see the show being filmed as a single-camera comedy. It will primarily appeal to adults, but it will also attract a family audience due to the characters' childlike qualities.

Pawnbroken - Episode Synopsis

EPISODE ONE – MY GIRL

One of Jim's two assistants announces he's leaving at the end of the week to travel. This leaves Jim with a headache. He needs to replace Carl as soon as possible as Patrick is due to go on his holiday, and Vanessa has shown a rare sense of altruism and has offered to work part-time, albeit her real reason is to keep an eye on her ex-husband, which horrifies Jim. He interviews three candidates, of which the final candidate, Natalie, is offered the post.

Vanessa makes a flying visit and asks Patrick to find out if Jim is seeing anyone as he has been behaving 'nicer' to her recently. Patrick also thinks he is, as he's overheard Jim on the phone to a female several times recently and has heard him promise to take the mystery woman to Brighton at the weekend. Patrick immediately regrets saying anything. Vanessa sweeps into the shop later in the day and spies Jim in an embrace with a younger woman. She storms around the counter and accuses him of being a cradle-snatcher, which is ironic as she is seeing a man 15 years her junior. The mystery woman turns around and reveals herself as their daughter, Lucy, who had come in to see her Dad.

Lucy is not impressed with her mother's outburst and walks out, with

Vanessa in tow, apologising profusely.

Carl explains to Patrick that this sort of scene is the reason he is delighted to be leaving.

EPISODE TWO – MAD WORLD

Jim gets mocked by two policemen when they observe him singing along to Kate Bush. Natalie starts her job and immediately makes an impression on her two male co-workers. She is about 15 years older than Patrick and 15 years younger than Jim. Her ex-boyfriend is trying to re-kindle their romance and is not getting the message that she's no longer interested.

Throughout the day, Vanessa constantly nags her ex-husband to finish the tax returns and deliver a new pair of slippers to his care-home-ridden mother. She also feels she must remind him of Lucy's operatic recital that evening, knowing Jim's forgetfulness provides him with the address. After a day of dealing with Vanessa and a series of exasperating customers, Jim is soothed by some kind words of solace from Natalie, which he assumes is because she has a thing for him. Driving to see his mother, he realises that he's left the slippers and the address of his daughter's performance, so he must swallow his pride and admit to Vanessa what she's done.

EPISODE THREE – ELECTRIC DREAMS

Jim is in a good mood as he has a date later on. He arrives at work, and immediately his happiness is destroyed. There's been a power cut, including the power to the safe timer. If he can't open the safe, he can't do business. He calls the engineer and is assured that he will be along presently. The engineer calls an hour later to explain that he's running late because his washing machine has broken and his kitchen is flooded. Jim is fuming, telling the others it's the worst excuse he's ever heard – akin to a schoolboy insisting he'd left his homework on the bus. The engineer finally turns up mid-morning as a potman delivers a parcel for Natalie from Kit, her ex. It's a pancake-maker. She's not impressed and gives it to Patrick, who is over the moon – that's his parent's anniversary present sorted.

Mrs Mullaney arrives outside with lunch for everybody. She is let in to sit down and begins to regale Natalie with some surprisingly frank stories of her love life. Natalie confides in her about Kit, and the old lady suggests she take what she can and have fun.

The engineer takes his time, and Jim fears that he won't make his date. Finally, the job is done, and he can open the shop. He calms down and looks forward to the evening. Later in the day, Jim receives a call. It's his date, and she tells him she has to cancel – her washing machine has overflowed and flooded the kitchen. As he is shutting the shop, the electricity goes down again, and Jim has to spend his evening in the cold, dark shop waiting for it to come back on.

EPISODE FOUR - HOT IN THE CITY

An unseasonably hot Autumn morning puts Jim in a worse mood than usual. Jim announces to Natalie that Vanessa revealed that she wants to sell her share of the business the day before. He is relieved that he won't have to deal with her again but is concerned that he has no idea who she'll sell to.

Elsewhere, Natalie's gifts sent from her ex, Kit, are getting ever more extravagant. This time, he sends a £200 Harrods gift card. Natalie hesitates to send it back this time.

Later on, Vanessa turns up unannounced again to drop the bombshell that her spendthrift friend, Vanessa and her husband, Trevor, have offered to buy her half of the business. Now Jim is worried that they'll be bankrupt in months if they are involved with the business. Along with the oppressive temperatures, this news leaves Jim frustrated and even more uncomfortable. A visit from Mrs Mullaney does little to improve matters, and neither does one from a middle-aged flirt, Mrs Spillett, who was always after Jim.

Aside from Jim's problems, George, the gossiping window cleaner, informs Jim that Patrick has been seen in a romantic clinch with a woman… an older woman. Throughout the day, every time Patrick serves a female, both Jim and Natalie debate and guess if *this* is the woman in question. Surely, it couldn't be Mrs Spillett?

Jim's mood picks up when, later on in the day, Vanessa phones him to sadly announce that Penelope has changed her mind and instead of buying into the business, and due to her assumption that global warming is hitting Southern England, she has decided she wants a swimming pool built in her garden instead.

On his way home, Jim spies Patrick with his mystery lady. He is astonished that the lady in question is none other than Mrs Spillett.

EPISODE FIVE – PARTY FEARS TWO

Before he even gets to work, he accidentally beeps his horn at a man in a wheelchair at a zebra crossing, and despite trying to voice his innocence, the disabled man doesn't want to know. A riled Jim says some unkind things to the man, although his attitude deserved them.

Vanessa has gone on holiday for a week, and Jim is happy she's out of his hair for a while. However, before she departs, she delivers a 50th birthday party invitation to Jim, which is to be hosted at her house. To compound his displeasure, Jim is expected to bring a 'plus one'. He assumes she only wants him there to humiliate him and any female he takes along, and so asks Natalie and Patrick for ideas to get out of it.

Kit tries harder to win Natalie back by sending her a piece of jewellery. She doesn't want it and plans to give it back to him. Jim decides he can't go to the party and try to think of a way out of it. Unfortunately, his daughter calls and begs him to go. He relents.

No, Jim has to find a suitable present that isn't too personal and isn't too expensive, but doesn't look too cheap. Natalie recommends he go to the discount perfume counter in a local pharmacy. , Towards the end of the day, Jim rushes out of the shop to buy the present but slips on the wet floor and damages his ankle. An ambulance is called, and Natalie accompanies him to the hospital. He is placed into a wheelchair but is relieved that he now has a proper excuse not to go to the party. However, his delight is swiftly curtailed when he sees a man on crutches walking toward him. It's the formerly wheelchair-bound man from the zebra crossing...

EPISODE SIX – TRUE COLOURS

Vanessa has decreed that the shop needs a make-over and arranges for a decorator to come in and paint it. Unfortunately, bottle green is not to Jim's or anyone else's taste. He wanted a lighter, mint green shade. The whole job is supposed to take a day and a half over the weekend. Jim tells George, the window cleaner, that he is getting the shop decorated, and he also dislikes the colour but promises to keep it a secret so as not to put off the customers. Jim is left scratching his head.

Kit steps up his attempts to win back Natalie, and finally, it appears to be working. His latest gift is a Gucci handbag, which arrives by courier. She loves Gucci handbags and has always dreamt of owning one. She messages Kit to thank him.

When the decorators arrive at midday, Jim shuts the shop and takes his staff to the pub for lunch.

Later on, when Jim goes back to his premises to see who the painters were getting on, he is delighted to know that they have used the wrong shade of green, which just happens to be his original preferred shade.

EPISODE SEVEN – LONELY THIS CHRISTMAS

It's Christmas Eve and the day of the staff Christmas dinner. Jim decides to take his employees to the local curry house. He's done well to keep Vanessa out of the picture, but dopey Patrick lets the cat out of the bag during one of Vanessa's regular early morning instruction phone calls.

Mrs Mullaney makes an appearance, gifting a Christmas cake that the staff is encouraged to slice and eat in front of her. It has the density of Patrick's brain, but she delights in their faux enjoyment of it.

Natalie tells the guys that she has forgiven kit and has decided to get back together with him. However, her parents disapprove and following an argument the night before, she decides to stay with him over Christmas. Jim is also not happy with her decision but chooses not to say anything, especially when the postman delivers a card to Natalie from Kit. Inside are the details of a mini-cruise he intends to take her on in the spring. His campaign of ever-increasing value gifts has done the trick.

With Jim, Natalie and Patrick already at the restaurant, Vanessa turns up fashionably late and explains that her young beau is on his way. She reveals that she is more than peeved that he has decided not to spend Christmas with her but with a friend's family instead. Eventually, he makes a grand entry, and we find out that Kit and Christopher are the same people due to the expression on his and Natalie's faces. She tells Jim, and initially, he delights in the idea of telling Vanessa, finally laying the killer blow to his ex-wife. However, to spare Natalie's feelings, he changes his mind. An uneasy meal takes place. Later on, knowing that Natalie has nowhere to go on Christmas Day, Jim builds up the courage to invite him to stay at his house and spend Christmas with him. Natalie accepts.

Pawnbroken - Character Biographies

MAIN CHARACTERS

JIM TRUEMAN– 50 years old. Cynical. Beholden to his ex-wife/silent business partner. Thinks of himself as a bit of a charmer, but can also be self-deprecating . His wit can be cutting and often gets him into trouble. Gets on with people most of the time, but is easily annoyed and frustrated by them. Forgetful, especially when under pressure. He likes to remind people he is in charge. Has been in the pawnbroking industry for 30 years. He dotes on his only daughter, Lucy. Lives alone in a two-bedroom flat. Often has conversations with himself when driving to and from work.

PATRICK BRUCE– 22. Good looking, slightly unkempt. A bit thick, but occasionally speaks more sense than anyone else. Very approachable and pliable. He likes to be seen as intelligent but is not, by spouting sayings and quotes he's seen or read. Some of Jim's bravado has rubbed off on him. Lives with parents and sister. Has GSCEs in Food tech and sociology and is a science fiction geek.

NATALIE REYES - 36. Attractive and slim. Extrovert and customer-friendly. Funny. She keeps her cards close to her chest and men on her side.Has just started working for Jim. Calm under pressure. Her ex-boyfriend, Kit, is always trying to get back with her by calling, texting, and sending ever more extravagant and gifts. She is continually rejecting his attempts to get back together. Is constantly flirting with Jim. Whether or not this is intentional to get what she wants is unknown.

VANESSA TRUEMAN – 49. Jim's ex-wife and current business partner. Always well made-up and dressed immaculately. Single-minded. Glamorous. Cutting and sarcastic, but inside, deep inside, has a heart. She has no faith at all in her ex-husband's abilities. Not at all, maternal. Has a new boyfriend, Christopher is many years her junior and wastes no opportunity to remind people of the fact.

PERIPHERAL RETURNING CHARACTERS

Mrs ELAINE MULLANEY – 80. Scatty, but kind-hearted customer, although she rarely does any business. She likes to feed 'her boys' with her spicy experimental food. Talks incessantly. Lives on her own. Her only social activity is visiting the shop. A former nurse. Claims to have no active tastebuds or a sense of smell.

GEORGE – 72. Window cleaner and local gossip. Delusions of grandeur. Irritable and lacks a sense of humour. Sees his profession as the fifth emergency service. No one is terribly interested in what he says but is compelled to offer a teaser of what he's seen. Often suggests that he could write a book on what he's seen through windows but is sure the contract he has with the council is part of the Official Secrets Act.

LUCY TRUEMAN – 18 . Pretty and intelligent. The only child of Jim and Vanessa. A Daddy's girl. Not on particularly good terms with her mother, with whom she lives. She is a talented opera singer and hopes that will be her career.

CARL JORDAN – 27. Shop assistant. Flighty and takes nothing seriously. Decides to leave the shop and go backpacking in Australia in episode 1. He is not seen again.

Episode 1 - My Girl

Written by Elliot Stanton

ACT ONE

ACT 1, SCENE 1; INT. JIM'S CAR [8.45 AM]

SHOT OF CAR CLOCK. IT SHOWS 8.45 AM

Looking very happy with himself, JIM waits at a red traffic light, he's singing along to The Eagles' 'Peaceful Easy Feeling' when he notices a small girl on a tricycle on the pavement.

JIM:
Hello. How are you, young lady? Where's your mummy?

The child simply stares at Jim for a moment before her mother appears from behind her immediately ushers her away. She turns around.

WOMAN:
Pervert!

JIM: (V.O.)

Charming. When did the world become a place when a 50-year old man can't smile and ask questions to a strange child from the safety of his car?

The lights change, Jim drives off.

FADE TO:

ACT 1, SCENE 2. EXT. FRONT OF SHOP [8.50 AM]

SHOT OF JIM'S WATCH. IT SHOWS 8.50

Jim walks up to the shop with keys in hand. CARL is waiting.

JIM:
Wonders will never cease. Here before the boss? I'm impressed.

CARL:
Morning Jim. I'd like a word with you before we open, please.

JIM:
(IGNORING HIM)Tell me, Carl, do I look like a pervert?

CARL:
Err, well, I'm no expert, Jim, but I've never had you down as a pervert. A bit of a letch, maybe.

JIM:
Really? But I'm not the sort of bloke to start eyeing up children on tricycles?

CARL:
I don't like where this is going. Have you had a visit from the police?

JIM:
What? No, no no. I'm just saying that it's a sad state of affairs when a simple, innocent gesture can be misconstrued as something sinister and malevolent.

CARL:
I don't really know what you're going on about, Jim, but I think you

should probably stop there. I don't want to aid and abet a crime.

CARL:

JIM:

No crime has been committed. It was just an innocent expression of concern when... oh, never mind. And thanks for the vote of confidence.

Jim raises the shutters, opens the door and enters the building. Carl follows.

CARL:

As I said, I want to tell you something.

JIM:

(STILL IGNORING CARL) No, I'm not going to let anything upset me today. I had some good news yesterday. My super-talented daughter has just been accepted to University Collage of Arts, London. Isn't that fantastic.Through all the upheaval of her parent's divorce and with all the nastiness coming from her mother's side, she's emerged the other side a strong, determined young lady with the voice of an angel.

CARL:

I'm delighted for you and Lucy, I really am, but I have to tell you something.

JIM:

Put the kettle on Carl. I think I've got some biscuits in my desk drawer.

An exasperated Carl walks into the kitchen and straight out again.

CARL:

I'm leaving, Jim.

JIM:

You're leaving Jim? Is he your boyfriend. And you named him after me; how sweet.

CARL:

No, I'm leaving. I'm going backpacking in Australia with an old college mate of mine.

Jim is taken aback and sits down on his swivel chair.

JIM:

Why? When was this decided? You're not in trouble with the law again with your...

Jim mimes smoking weed.

CARL:

What? No. I just want a change of scenery and this opportunity arose. I don't want to waste my life working as an assistant in a shop. No offence.

JIM:

None taken, I'm sure. Are you sure the police aren't after you for any other reason?

CARL:

If you mean, have I been caught eyeing-up toddlers on bikes from my car - then the answer is 'no.'

JIM:

That's not funny. Anyway, it was trike. So, when are you thinking of leaving? At the end of the month?

CARL:

No, at the end of the week. And I am leaving. There's no thinking to be

EPISODE 1 - MY GIRL

done.

JIM:
This *week*? How am I going to find someone else in such a short time?

There's a knock on the front door; it's PATRICK. Jim unlocks the door and lets him in.

PATRICK:
Good morning everyone.

JIM:
Good? What's good about it? I mean, it started good. It started very good indeed until I was callously accused of being a pervert and then I found out my staff numbers will be reduced by 50% on Friday week.

PATRICK:
Pervert? Who said that, and what did you do?

JIM:
Oh, don't worry about that. That's the least of my worries. Carl has decided that working at Trueman's doesn't fulfill him anymore and wants to bum around Australia with an old boyfriend.

CARL:
(TO JIM) Friend, not boyfriend. (TO PATRICK) It's just an old college mate of mine.

Jim re-takes his seat and stuffs a chocolate digestive in his mouth. Patrick peers at the yearly calendar on the wall.

PATRICK:

Jim, I don't want to make things worse, but you are aware that I'm on holiday from next Monday.

JIM:

Oh, this just gets better and better. Do you know what will happen now, gentlemen? Do you know what you have just done to me?

Patrick and Carl look at Jim. They are confused.

JIM: (CONT'D)

If I can't find a replacement quickly, I'll have to ask Vanessa to step in. My ex-wife who stole my house, my car and half of my business. Remember? She hates me and she hates it here, but she'll do it just to spite me and make out she's doing me a favour.

You've seen what she's like in the five-minute bursts of seething nastiness when she pops in to harangue and harass me. Can you imagine nine hours of it- every day? Oh my God, what have you done to me? I'm a broken man. A broken man, I tell you. She started chipping away, and you've just finished me off. I won't be able to continue in that environment. I'll have to close the shop and move out of my pokey two-bedroom flat into a dingy one-bedroom flat. I can imagine setting the cockroach traps even now. Calm down, Jim. Come on, let's get open while I still have a business.

PATRICK and CARL: (MOUTHING TO EACH OTHER)

Cockroach traps?

GEORGE, the window cleaner stands in the open doorway.

GEORGE:

Tut Tut. That's a security issue.

CARL:

Hello George. Would you say that Jim looks like a pervert?

EPISODE 1 - MY GIRL

Carl and Patrick high-five each other and start giggling like children.

GEORGE:

I take it from your infantile behaviour, that was supposed to be an attempt to sully your boss's good name, albeit in a barely humorous way?

JIM:

Thank you, George.

GEORGE:

You need to take these two in hand, Jim. When I was young, if I tried to make a joke at the expense of my guv'nor, he would have kicked my arse all the way down the road before giving me my cards.

JIM:

(TO PATRICK & CARL) You two, open the safe and prepare to open the shop.

The two assistants run off, still giggling.

GEORGE:

You're not, are you?

JIM:

Not what?

GEORGE:

A pervert?

JIM:

(angrily) No. Insolent boy, that Carl. You know, he's told me he's leaving at the end of the week. Dropped it on me not five minutes ago.

GEORGE:
Really? Nothing to do with… (LEANS IN AND WHISPERS) you being a pervert, is it?

JIM:
I'm not a bloody pervert, okay?

Several pedestrians stare at Jim as they walk by.

JIM: (CONT'D.)
Haven't you got some windows to clean?

Jim storms off. George shakes his head and slaps his squeegee on the window.

FADE TO:

ACT 1, SCENE 3; INT. BEHIND SHOP COUNTER [9.30 AM]

SHOT OF THE BOTTOM OF THE TIME ON COMPUTER SCREEN. IT SHOWS 9.30 PM

Carl is serving a customer while Jim stands back leaning against the wall, in a world of his own.

CARL:
I've tested it, but this bangle isn't gold. However, the ring is, and I can offer you £30.

EPISODE 1 - MY GIRL

CUSTOMER #1:

But you said you'd give me £120.

CARL:

If the bangle was real…

CUSTOMER #1:

It is real. It's a real bangle, love.

CARL:

I meant if it was real gold.

CUSTOMER #1:

So, can you do £80?

CARL:

No, I can lend you £30 for the ring. That's all, sir.

CUSTOMER #1:

But I paid twenty quid for that bangle.

CARL:

With all due respect, sir, how can you expect it to be real gold if you paid just £20? Where did you buy it? (TO JIM) Off a bloke in a pub or a bloke on the street?

CUSTOMER #1:

I bought it from a bloke in the street. I know him from the pub. He's a sound geezer.I tell you what mate, give me £50 for the pair of them, and we'll all be happy.

Carl is exasperated, so Jim steps in.

JIM:

What my colleague has tried to explain to you, sir, is that due to the bangle not being gold, in any way, shape, or form, we can't take it at all. It has no value.

CUSTOMER #1:

Oh, piss off!

The customer snatches back his jewellery and storms out.

JIM:

What a character, eh? You won't find local colour like that in Australia. Do you really want to give up all this - all this banter and bonne homie to muck around for a few months on the other side of the planet with someone you barely know? You do realise, he could be some kind of psychopath? This could all be a ruse to satisfy a desire… a compunction he's had all his life for murder. He could creep up behind you, slit your throat and leave your sorry carcass in the middle of the Outback for the rabid dingoes to pick over?

You do know that, don't you?

Carl doesn't answer because someone enters the shop. A slim, attractive woman in her mid-30s walks up to the counter. Jim perks up and barges past Carl to serve her. Carl walks off.

JIM: (CONT'D)

Good morning madam. How may I be of assistance?

NATALIE:

Hi. I'm looking to sell a ring and wanted to know if you'd be interested in buying it from me?

JIM:

I'll certainly have a look at it for you.

NATALIE places the single stone diamond ring under the window.

NATALIE:

It was an engagement ring. I won't be needing it any more.
Jim picks up the ring and looks it over through his loupe.

JIM:

It's a nice piece, alright. A very nice piece. Have you any idea what you want for it?

NATALIE:

Not really. I just want rid of it.

JIM:

(UNDER HIS BREATH) Is the right answer. (TO NATALIE) I see. Well, as I said, it's a nice ring, and the stone is a beauty. However, the pear-shaped diamond is not a terribly popular cut these days. Also, there are a few inclusions and a couple of claws need building- up.

NATALIE:

I know. I used to work in the trade myself.

JIM:

(UNDER HIS BREATH) Oh shit. (TO NATALIE) Really -locally?

NATALIE:

No, my uncle owned a jewellery shop in West London. It was a family business, and with any family business, especially an Italian family, things often got heated, so I got out a couple of years ago and I moved to North London.

JIM:

So, are you working at the moment?

NATALIE:

I'm doing a bit of freelance photography work, but it's not a regular income.

JIM:

I see. Well, I've looked over your ring and I'd be happy to offer you £600.

NATALIE:

That's not bad at all. Do you mind if I think about it and maybe pop back later on?

JIM:

Not at all.

Jim hands back the ring to Natalie, and she exits the shop. Carl enters the scene, casually eating an apple.

CARL:

Lives locally? Not in regular employment Has worked in the business before? Nice manner?

JIM:

Oh, bugger.

Jim rushes around the counter and runs out of the shop to find Natalie, but she is nowhere to be seen.

END OF ACT 1

ACT 2

ACT 2, SCENE 1; INT. OFFICE [12 PM]

SHOT OF JIM'S WATCH. IT'S MIDDAY.

Jim is sitting at his desk with his head in his hands. He's been moping around all morning. Carl and Patrick watch him from the doorway.

PATRICK:
Do you still think she'll come back?

JIM:
Oh, I don't know. I hoped she would have returned by now. I offered her a really good price. She won't get anywhere near that from anyone else around here. Why did I not click?

CARL:
I have to say that you surprised me. I thought you'd offer her the job straight away. She was offering herself on a plate - excuse the innuendo.

JIM:
Then why didn't you run out and alert me?

CARL:
It's not my place, Jim. Besides, how was I supposed to know you'd be so slow on the uptake?

JIM:
There's no doubt about it; I'm going to have to go cap in hand to Vanessa now and beg her to come to work. Boy, that's going to be a conversation and a half. Oh, she'll make me beg; mark my words. Having to go to that woman who literally bled me dry… who thrust her hand into my chest and ripped out my bleeding heart… that witch who took away everything I worked my life for and left me…

CARL:
Broken?

JIM:
Yes. Broken. God, I hate that hex. Do you know something? I've bitten my lip for too long. It's time I told her exactly how I feel. If she thinks she can ride roughshod all over me for one moment longer, she can…

Jim's mobile rings on the desk. Jim jumps as he sees its VANESSA. He stares at the ringing phone, eventually answering it.

JIM: (CONT'D)
Hello Vanessa. I couldn't get to my phone immediately as I was a little busy. I run a shop, you see… No, I'm not being facetious. Yes, I know you're a busy woman too… Are you? Yes, I'll be here. I'll see you in a few minutes. Bye Vanessa… Yes, I'll make sure I'm not busy. Oh, by the way, I have to tell you that Carl is… (PAUSES) She hangs up.

EPISODE 1 - MY GIRL

CARL:

Well, you certainly put her in her place, Jim.

JIM:

Now is not the time, Carl. Patrick!

Patrick enters the office.

JIM: (CONT'D)

Will you tidy this place up. It's a pigsty. You might be happy living like this, but I'm not, okay?

PATRICK:

(TO CARL)Vanessa's on her way in, isn't she?

CARL:

Yup.

Carl and Patrick begin to tidy up the office, and Jim goes back to sitting at his desk with his head in his hands.

FADE TO:

ACT 2, SCENE 2; INT. SHOP. [12.15 PM]

SHOT ON WALL CLOCK. IT SHOWS 12.15 PM

Patrick and Carl continue cleaning the office while Jim serves, MR ROUGH, an unkept-looking customer.

MR ROUGH:

The name's 'ROUGH.' Rough by name, rough by nature, eh?

Mr Rough laughs like its the funniest thing he's ever said.

JIM:
That's quite a self-endorsement.

MR ROUGH:
You can't make a silk purse out of a sow's ear, as my wife used to say.

JIM:
Was she...

MR ROUGH:
Rough? She was when she married me.

Mr Rough laughs even harder.

MR ROUGH: (CONT'D)
Ironically, she was Primm, before she married. That was her maiden name, not a character description. Although she was an elegant woman, she didn't mind slumming it. That's what first attracted me.

JIM:
Yes, quite. Anyway, I can lend you £300 on your bracelet.

Jim picks up a gents identity bracelet of the scales and places it on the counter in front of him.

MR ROUGH:
One hundred will be enough. I just need some money to buy a new suit for a special occasion. My son's in court next Tuesday, and I want to look the part.

Mr Rough looks very proud. Jim looks at him in disbelief.

JIM:

One hundred pounds for a new suit?

MR ROUGH:

Well, its a bit more than I usually spend on new clobber, but as I said, it's a special occasion.

JIM:

Fascinating. So, you're no longer together with your wife?

MR ROUGH:

Nah. We split up a few years ago. We just grew apart. Although we were similar in many ways, it was the little differences that created resentment. I liked going out to the casino all night; she didn't. I liked watching sport all weekend, she didn't. I cut my toenails in bed; she didn't. We did have things in common though - I like women; and so did she - and that was the clincher. There was never much of a future after that revelation.

Pity really . She was a classy lady. She's the sort of person who would only piss in the bath at the end of a soak if you know what I mean?

JIM:

How delightful. Now if you'd just like to sign in the boxes on all three sheets.

Jim hands his uncouth customer the contracts to sign.

MR ROUGH:

Are you married yourself?

JIM:

Not now. We divorced three years ago. We had a few little differences too - the main one being that we hated each other. She's still my business partner, but I don't see her that often thankfully.

The front door swings open and in walks VANESSA. She is dressed immaculately in a designer dress, fresh from the hairdressers.

VANESSA:
James, we need to talk about the outgoings. I see your busy, so I'll be in the office.

Vanessa sweeps through the shop and rounds the counter, disappearing into the office.

MR ROUGH:
Wow. Speak of the devil. Eh?

JIM:
You don't know how accurate you are.

Jim hands Mr Rough his money and puts his pawn away before entering the office. Vanessa is sitting at his desk. Carl is at lunch and Patrick is in the kitchen.

VANESSA:
When were you going to tell me?

JIM:
Tell you what?

VANESSA:
Tell me that Carl is leaving on Saturday and Patrick is going on holiday next week. Honestly, James, run a business? I don't think you could run a bath?

JIM:
(UNDER HIS BREATH) At least I wouldn't piss in it.

EPISODE 1 - MY GIRL

VANESSA:

So, we'll need someone to step in, won't we

JIM:

Yes.

VANESSA:

And I suppose you wanted to ask me?

JIM:

If you're not too busy with the hairdressers, the manicurists and the Reiki head massages .

VANESSA:

I'll ignore that and I'll save you that humbling experience of asking me. I'll do it. It might even be fun.

JIM:

Fun

VANESSA:

Okay - wrong choice of word. I can't imagine doing anything with you as 'fun', but hopefully it won't be half as agonising as your face suggests it might.

Jim forces a smile. He doesn't know now to react.

VANESSA: (CONT'D)

I might even ask Penelope to come and help too. Now that WILL be fun.

Jim looks absolutely horrified.

JIM:

No, you can't ask her. She's an absolute disaster. We'll have no customers left if she's left to deal with them.

VANESSA:

What nonsense. She's very good with people, and besides, she's my best friend. We used to do everything together. And she's worked in retail before. I'm sure she'll jump at the chance.

JIM:

Worked in retail? Only in the sense that she's spent longer in Harvey Nicholls than most of their staff. She has no sense of worth and spends money like it's going out of fashion. More fool Stuart for supplying her with the funds to fritter away on £300 belts and £500 handbag tags and heaven knows what else.

VANESSA:

At least her husband loves her enough to furnish her lifestyle.

JIM:

Oh, don't start. I gave you enough.

VANESSA:

You didn't - the divorce court did.

JIM:

Lucy? Our incredible daughter who I encouraged and nurtured - who has now being accepted to UCA?

Vanessa is about to launch into a tirade when Patrick exits the kitchen with a cup of tea for Vanessa.

PATRICK:

Tea's up!

EPISODE 1 - MY GIRL

VANESSA:

And not a moment too soon.

JIM:

So, me you and Penelope - that'll be quite the experience.

VANESSA:

Oh, stop being such an old misery. It'll work out just fine. I wouldn't invite her if I thought she'd be a disaster. I do own half of the business, don't forget.

JIM:

I'm hardly likely to forget that, am I?

VANESSA:

Do you want my help or are you happy to see the business fold? - because, James, I am certainly not. If you'd excuse me, I have a few phone calls to make.

Jim leaves Vanessa to it and joins Patrick behind the counter in the shop.

FADE TO:

ACT 2, SCENE 3; INT. SHOP. [12.45 PM]

SHOT OF WALL CLOCK. IT SHOWS 12.45.

An 80-year old woman enters the shop. Patrick is kneeling down

unboxing printer paper.

MRS MULLANEY:
Cooey, Jimmy! Is anyone there?

Patrick springs up in front of MRS MULLANEY, causing her to jump back.

MRS MULLANEY: (CONT'D)
Oh, goodness me, Patrick. You startled me. I almost dropped your lunch.

PATRICK:
I'm sorry about that, Mrs. Mullaney. My lunch?

Jim enters the scene.

JIM:
Hello Elaine. How are you today?

MRS MULLANEY:
Oh fine, fine. You look rather red-faced and flustered though. Is it your blood pressure again?

JIM:
My blood pressure? What's wrong with my blood pressure? Who told you about my blood pressure?

PATRICK:
(INTERRUPTING) Mrs Mullaney has bought us in lunch...again.

MRS MULLANEY:
You know how I like to look after my boys. I hate to think of you going hungry. Here, I've made you this.

EPISODE 1 - MY GIRL

Mrs Mullaney takes out a sealed Tupperware box and puts it in the drawer under the window.

PATRICK:

What have we got today - and is it spicy?

MRS MULLANEY:

Its tandoori chicken, boys, but with a little kick.

JIM:

A little kick to my lower regions that could confine me to the little boys' room for the rest of the day and beyond, eh Elaine?

MRS MULLANEY:

Oh, stop it. I know you're just teasing. Look, I can't stop long; just try a bit before I go. I want to see you enjoy it.

JIM:

Go on Patrick, do what Mrs Mullaney says.

PATRICK:

Why me?

JIM:

Why me?', he says. Because, Patrick, I know that tandoori chicken is your favourite.

PATRICK:

Is it?

JIM:

Of course, it is, if you want a job to come back to after your holiday, you'll try a nice big mouthful.

Patrick gingerly takes the top of the Tupperware box off at arms length and carefully tears off a piece of chicken.

JIM: (CONT'D)
Come on, pick up a leg and have a nice big bite. Surely you want to experience the myriad of delicate flavours that Mrs Mullaney has slaved for hours adding just for us.

A defeated Patrick, sneers at Jim and picks up a well-coated leg and takes a bite.

MRS MULLANEY:
Well - what do you think?

As the intense heat builds up in his mouth, Patrick's face turns crimson and his eyes begin to tear up.

JIM:
Yes, what do you think, Patrick - is it as delicious as it looks?

PATRICK:
(BARELY ABLE TO GET HIS WORDS OUT) It's…it's quite exceptional, Mrs Mullaney. (TO JIM) I need to make Vanessa her tea.

JIM:
Really? I thought you just made one for her.

PATRICK:
No, I think she really wants one right now.

Jim overdramatically peers through the doorway into the office. Vanessa is on the phone with a mug of tea in front of her.

JIM:
Nope. You really did. I can see it in front of her.

Jim glories in Patrick's discomfort. Mrs Mullaney smiles innocently, believing that he loves her food. Patrick can't stand it any longer.

PATRICK:
I'm going to lunch!

Patrick runs off into the office. Jim and Mrs Mullaney look at each other, smiling as we hear a running tap and a series of gasps and loud moans coming from the kitchen. Vanessa appears.

VANESSA:
What have you done to Patrick?

JIM:
He was trying some of Mrs Mullaney's tandoori chicken. I don't think he's used to a little bit of spice. Why don't you try some, dear?

Vanessa eyes up the box of chicken, looks at Mrs Mullaney, and then at Jim.

VANESSA:
No. And don't call me dear.

Vanessa spins around and returns to the office. Jim replaces the lid on the box.

JIM:
Some people have no sense of adventure, Elaine.

MRS MULLANEY:
Anyway, I must be off now, Jimmy. I need to get back home to watch Judge Rinder. Oh, he's a dish. If I was 30 years younger.

Mrs Mullaney giggles and walks to the front door.

JIM:
(UNDER HIS BREATH) 30 years?And the rest. Mind you; I don't think the age difference would be your biggest stumbling block, Elaine.

Jim walks into the office. Patrick can still be heard gargling and spluttering in the kitchen. Jim ignores him and focuses on Vanessa, who is standing up behind his desk with her coat on.

VANESSA:
That's sorted then. Georgie will be delighted to help us out. So, from Monday week, it'll be me, you and Georgie.

JIM:
Unless I take on someone else in the meantime.

VANESSA:
James, you still have two boxes of your adolescent filth you've yet to find time to pick up from my spare room for the last three years, so I doubt very much if you'll be able to find someone suitable in such a short space of time.

JIM:
Firstly, Vanessa, it's not filth; they are collector's editions of well established and well-respected gentlemen's magazines. They're full of interesting and well-written articles, vintage advertisements and…

EPISODE 1 - MY GIRL

PATRICK: (FROM THE KITCHEN)
Tits.

VANESSA:
Precisely. Filth. Right, I'm off. I shall see you on Monday at 9 o'clock sharp. I'm sure I'll speak to you in the meantime.

JIM:
I'm sure you will.

Vanessa sweeps out of the shop. Jim sits down on his vacated chair. Patrick enters the office.

JIM:
Thanks for that.

PATRICK:
You deserved it after subjecting me to that burning hell.

JIM:
Touché.

They both look at the box of Tandoori chicken.

JIM: (CONT'D)
Right, bag it up and dispose of it in the bin out front. I don't want it on my desk, in case it escapes and eats through my beautiful desk.

PATRICK:
It's always me who has to do the donkey work.

JIM:
Durr. Me, boss; you, donkey. Come on and get on with it.

Patrick places the Tupperware box in a plastic bag and takes it out of the shop. Jim reverts to his head in hands pose and sighs loudly.

END OF ACT TWO

ACT 3

ACT 3, SCENE 1; INT. SHOP [2.30 PM]

SHOT OF CUSTOMER'S POCKET WATCH BEFORE HE HANDS IT TO CARL FOR APPRAISAL. IT SHOWS 2.30 PM.

CUSTOMER #2:
Well, what do you think?

CARL:
It's a beauty.

CUSTOMER #2:
It's been in the family for generations, and it's all original, including the chain.

Carl notices an inscription on the back of the watch case. It was presented to 'R. Wickramarante for 30 years of outstanding service at Tate & Lyle's'.

CARL:
Sir, when you say it's been in the family for generations, whose family are you referring to exactly?

EPISODE 1 - MY GIRL

CUSTOMER #2:

My family, why?

CARL:

It's just that you don't look like a 'Wickramarante'.

CUSTOMER #2:

Ah, well, my mother's Indian.

CARL:

It's a Sri Lankan name.

CUSTOMER #2:

I meant the Indian subcontinent.

CARL:

So your mother was Sri Lankan.

CUSTOMER #2:

Yes. Her family came over here in 1945, and she married my Dad in 1946. It was a whirlwind romance.

CARL:

It must have been.

CUSTOMER #2:

What do you mean?

CARL:

You must take after your father's side of the family - what with the red hair, freckles, and blue eyes.

CUSTOMER #2:

I guess so.

CARL:

And your mother was quite a lady. She must have made the news when she had you?

CUSTOMER #2:

I don't understand.

CARL:

She married in 1946, yes?

CUSTOMER #2:

Yes

CARL:

So, she was at least 18.

CUSTOMER #2:

I suppose so.

CARL:

Then she must have given birth to you when she was close to 70. That's quite a feat. Unless, of course, your youthful looks disguise the sad reality that you're an old age pensioner.

CUSTOMER #2:

Are you calling me a liar?

CARL:

I really don't want to offend a customer, but weighing everything up and forgetting my manners for a moment and also bearing in mind that I'm leaving this place at the end of the week - yes, you're a liar.

EPISODE 1 - MY GIRL

CUSTOMER #2:

I'm outraged.

CARL:

To be fair, that is the sort of thing a sexagenarian might say. Come on, mate; you've been rumbled. Now, I have two choices - I can hold on to the watch and call the police, or I could hand it back to you and you can try your luck somewhere else.

The customer waits and thinks for a moment before panicking and turns around to leave the shop.

CARL: (CONT'D)

(TO HIMSELF) I didn't reckon on that option.

He takes the pocket watch to show Jim who is doing some paperwork.

JIM:

That's a beauty.

CARL:

I know. That's what I thought. Nicked though.

JIM:

Oh no, you didn't lend on it, did you?

CARL:

No, of course not. The guy knew I rumbled him and scarpered.

JIM:

The idiot. 18ct carat, fully hallmarked - It's got to be worth a grand of anyone's money.

CARL:
Are you going to report it to the police?

JIM:
Of course, but not now. I'll do it when I get the time.

Jim puts the watch in his desk drawer and out of the same drawer takes a packet of biscuits. He pops one in his mouth. Carl stands, watching him. Someone else walks into the shop.

JIM: (CONT'D)
Carl…customer.

Carl goes to meet the customer and when he's out of sight, Jim takes the watch from the drawer to take a close look.

JIM: (CONT'D)
(TO HIMSELF) It really is a lovely piece. Tell you what Jim, if miracles happen and Natalie walks back through that door, sells me her ring and takes the job I'll offer her…I'll report it to the police. If not…this baby's mine.

The phone rings and Jim picks up.

JIM: (CONT'D)
(ON PHONE) Oh, hello, Mrs Shah… Yes, Mrs Shah, the redemption fee is the same as last week… No, Mrs Shah, I won't sell it. You still have a month left on your contract… Yes, Mrs Shah, I promise…No, Patrick's at lunch, but he'd tell you exactly the same. This is Jim; Jim Trueman…Yes, Mrs Shah, I know exactly what I'm talking about. It's my business… No, Mrs Shah, Carl is with a customer, but I can assure you, everyone here will tell you the same thing - your pledge is absolutely, definitely and without a shadow of a doubt safe…Yes, it's IN the safe too. Goodbye, Mrs Shah. Goodbye.

EPISODE 1 - MY GIRL

Patrick returns from his lunch.

PATRICK:

Mrs Shah, again?

JIM:

Not much gets past you, does it, son?

PATRICK:

What does she think we're doing with her jewellery? If she doesn't trust us, then why does she keep coming back to us?

JIM:

She's just a bit neurotic. Most women are.

PATRICK:

That's a bit of a wild generalisation, isn't it?

JIM:

Okay then, women that I know.

PATRICK:

Perhaps that's more of a reflection on you, if I'm honest.

JIM:

Patrick, I don't pay you to be honest. Well, I do, but...

PATRICK:

(INTERRUPTS) *"As women, we are more than our looks, weight, clothes, or our partner."*

JIM:

What??

PATRICK:

It's a quote.

JIM:

Another one of the quotes you've seen in a magazine or on a poster that bares little or no connection to what we're talking about, I suppose. Hmmm, let me guess - Germaine Greer? Oprah Winfrey? Margaret Thatcher?

PATRICK:

Actually, it was Scarlett Moffatt.

JIM:

Of course, it was. (SIGHS) Of course, it was.

FADE TO:

ACT 3, SCENE 2. INT. SHOP. [4 PM]

SHOT OF ORNAMENTAL DESK CLOCK. IT SHOWS 4 PM.

Jim has just returned from the gents. Carl and Patrick are behind the counter with a surprise for Jim.

CARL:

There's a lady here to see you.

JIM:

Not again. Isn't once a day enough? What does she want now?

NATALIE:

Do you talk about all your customers like that?

EPISODE 1 - MY GIRL

JIM:

Natalie!? Oh, I'm so sorry. I thought it was my wife.

NATALIE:

Is your wife in her 30s with a gym- ready body and eyes you can get lost in?

Jim, now standing in front of Natalie, stops in his tracks and stares trance-like into Natalie's hazel eyes in wonderment like a lovelorn teenager.

JIM:

(STUTTERING) Err, no. Definitely not. Err..

Carl and Patrick giggle behind him. This breaks Jim's trance and he turns to them.

JIM: (CONT'D)

Haven't you two got work to do? Patrick, clean the toilet and Carl, you can sweep the floor in the shop.

PATRICK:

(TO HIMSELF) Why do I get all the crappy jobs?

The two boys attend to their tasks. Jim attends to Natalie.

NATALIE:

I've thought about your offer for the ring, and I'd like to accept it, please.

JIM:

Excellent. You don't want to hang onto it anyway; being reminded of your ex-boyfriend all the time.

NATALIE:

True.

Jim prepares the receipt for Natalie to sign. She signs, and Jim hands over the money.

NATALIE: (CONT'D)

Thanks. It'll come in very handy. I'll be seeing you then.

JIM:

One minute. I'm glad you came back. Not only to buy your jewellery, but I wanted to ask you a question.

NATALIE:

Jim, I'm flattered. You don't hang around, do you? I've just split up with my fella.

JIM:

What? No no no. That's not what I meant.

Jim pauses, weighing up Natalie's flirty comment.

JIM: (CONT'D)

What I wanted to ask is that if you are still looking for work, I wonder if you'd like to work here. I mean, you don't have to give me an answer straight away - you might not want to work in a shop again.

It can be a bit dull, and the customers can be very trying...

NATALIE: (INTERRUPTS)

Yes.

EPISODE 1 - MY GIRL

JIM:

I know it's not the most glamourous of positions, and you'll be expected to work most Saturdays, but it's a job and with the economy as it is any income is better than none.

NATALIE:

Jim, I said 'yes'. I'd like to accept your offer of employment.

JIM:

Oh. Oh, well that's great. Can you start on Monday?

NATALIE:

Yes, I can. I'll bring my P60 with me then, shall I?

JIM:

Yes, that's fine.

Once again, Jim stands not knowing what to do.

NATALIE:

Aren't you going to come around the counter and shake my hand to welcome me to the company? I'm afraid I don't kiss on a first date.

Jim nervously laughs before doing what he was told and joins Natalie on the other side of the counter and shakes her hand, warmly. He holds on to her hand.

JIM:

So, Monday then.

NATALIE:

Monday it is.

JIM:

9 o'clock?

NATALIE:

9 o'clock.

JIM:

I look forward to it.

NATALIE:

I'll need my hand back if I'm going to spend my money on some new work clothes.

JIM:

Yes, of course.

Carl leans on his broom, sniggering at the comical scene. Jim releases Natalie's hand.

NATALIE:

Bye, Jim… and thanks.

JIM:

No, thank you. You've saved me from a fate worse than death.

Natalie smiles at Jim and leaves the shop.

JIM: (CONT'D)

Oh, thank heavens for that. Carl, get some money out of petty cash and go and buy a bottle of champagne.

CARL:

Champagne?

EPISODE 1 - MY GIRL

JIM:

Well, a bottle of Prosecco. We're going to celebrate. It's a joyous day. (PAUSES) Hold on, I'm not sure if we should be drinking alcohol at work.

CARL:

We could make it my leaving drink, I suppose?

JIM:

Good idea. Chop chop…oh, and fetch Patrick from the khazi. And tell him to wash his hands.

CARL:

Will do, boss.

JIM:

And before we toast my reprieve… and your imminent departure, I shall call Vanessa and explain, very nicely, that her services will no longer be required.

Jim stands in the open shop doorway with his hands on his hips, barely able to stop smiling.

FADE TO:

ACT 3, SCENE 3. INT. OFFICE. [4.15 PM]

SHOT OF THE CLOCK ON THE PHONE. IT SHOWS 4.15 PM.

The three men sit in the office with a mug of Prosecco each. Jim dials Vanessa's phone number and puts her on speakerphone. Vanessa answers.

JIM:

Hello Vanessa.

VANESSA:

Yes, what is it?

JIM:

About next week…

VANESSA:

It's been arranged. I told you.

JIM:

I'm calling you to say that you don't need to come in now. Or Penelope, for that matter.

VANESSA:

Oh, don't tell me that silly boy has changed his mind about leaving. He doesn't know what he's doing from one minute to the next. If I were you, I'd tell him…

Jim quickly picks up the receiver. Carl looks surprised.

EPISODE 1 - MY GIRL

JIM:
No, no. He's still going. In actual fact, I've taken someone on. Someone who lives locally; has previous experience in the business, and who has a winning personality.

VANESSA:
Oh I get it. Pretty, is she?

JIM:
That's not the reason I employed her.

VANESSA:
So, she is then?

JIM:
So what if she is? What does that have to with anything. You are not my keeper, Vanessa. Not anymore, anyway.

VANESSA:
I just hope she knows what she's getting in to. I'll keep my diary free, just in case she changes her mind.

JIM:
She won't. Goodbye Vanessa.

Jim slams down the phone in indignation.

JIM: (CONT'D)
God, that woman knows how to suck every bit of joy out of my life. She's left me a...

PATRICK:
Broken man; yes, we know. Just be grateful she won't be coming in to

work.

JIM:

Yes, I suppose so. Things could have gone much, much worse today.

Jim opens his drawer and takes out his biscuits. He notices the pocket watch and picks it up.

JIM: (CONT'D)

(TO HIMSELF) Ah well, a deal's a deal. I'll report it tomorrow.

FADE TO:

ACT 3, SCENE 4. INT. JIMS CAR. [5.45 PM]

SHOT OF THE CAR CLOCK. IT SHOWS 5.45 PM.

Jim is in his car, waiting at a red light. He notices a man of his age walking arm-in-arm with a woman considerably younger than himself. She is attractive and he is certainly not. They're smiling and chatting.

JIM: (V.O.)

There's nothing wrong with that. So what if a young lady prefers the more mature gentleman? Even if he does look like something that's fallen from the masonry of Notre Dame Cathedral. It happens all the time nowadays. Besides, I'm better looking than him, I have all my own teeth, and I have my own business (well, half of one). This could be a sign. Perhaps Natalie could be the one.

A young, good-looking man approaches them and the girl hugs him. They kiss on the lips. She kisses the older man on the cheek, and he waves them off. The woman spies Jim staring at her.

WOMAN #2:

Pervert!

The lights change to green, and Jim drives off in a state of shock. He glances in the rearview mirror.

JIM: (V.O.)

Have I got 'pervert' written on my forehead or something? Maybe my photo is up on trees and lampposts around here with the warning - 'Pervert At Large'?

No, I'm not going to let that notion spoil my day. What could have been a disaster has worked out pretty damned well. It could be a fresh start for this broken man.

SHOT OF JIM'S CAR DRIVING AWAY DOWN A LEAFY SUBURBAN STREET.

END OF ACT. END OF EPISODE

Episode 2 - Mad World

Written by Elliot Stanton

EPISODE 2 - MAD WORLD

ACT 1

ACT 1, SCENE 1 INT. CAR [8.45AM]

SHOT OF CAR CLOCK. IT'S 8.45 AM

JIM waits at traffic lights. He is singing along to Kate Bush's Wuthering Heights with his window down and notices a police car in the adjacent lane. The two occupants are staring at him in amusement. He stops singing and turns the music off.

JIM:
(UNDER HIS BREATH)Come on. Come on. Change. Always red; never, ever green. Why are you always red, you bastards?

The policemen start to laugh. They know Jim is aware of their presence.

POLICEMAN:
(LAUGHING) Come on, don't be shy; you're not bad. In fact, that's the finest falsetto I've heard since 'Staying Alive.'

JIM: (V.O.)
It couldn't have been Bowie or Sinatra, could it? Oh no, it had to be Kate bloody Bush. Still red? Come on, change, damn you.

The other copper gives him 'double finger guns' before they drive off..

JIM:
(SHOUTING AT THE DEPARTED POLICE CAR) Yeah, yeah. It wasn't like I was singing 'I Am What I Am' or 'I Will Survive, was it?'

Jim turns the radio up again. 'I Fought The Law' by The clash is now playing.

JIM: (CONT'D)
They wouldn't have been so mocking if I was belting out this. I fought the law and the sodding law won alright.

A few minutes later, Jim parks his car in a car port at the rear of his shop. His phone rings.

JIM:
(INTO PHONE) Yes, VANESSA… It's the very first thing on my schedule… Yes, of course, I realise how important it is to complete the tax return on time… I'm on it… No, you don't have to remind me again! Okay, I must go. Goodbye Vanessa.

FADE TO:

ACT 1, SCENE 2. INT. PAWN SHOP OFFICE [9 AM]

SHOT OF PATRICK'S WATCH. IT SHOWS 9 O' CLOCK.

PATRICK is on the landline in the back office as Jim enters the premises from the back door.

PATRICK:
(INTO PHONE) Yes, Vanessa. I'll be sure to remind him. Yes…yes, and I'll tell him that too. Err, Vanessa, I think it might be best if you told him

that yourself. Okay. Bye, Vanessa.

JIM:
What does she want now? I just literally got off the phone to her.

PATRICK:
You cut her off. Anyway, she said you should do the tax return online as it's so much easier. She fears they won't be able to read your 'incomprehensible scrawl?'

JIM:
I don't believe that woman. She's crucifying me, Patrick. I'm going to fill in the forms by hand, as I do every year, quite successfully, and quite legibly, I might add. I don't like filling out forms online, because you can't always go back to check for errors. You know something, Patrick, she's left me a broken man.

PATRICK:
I know. I know. She also wanted to remind you about Lucy's recital tonight, and that you are expected to go.

JIM:
I'm fully aware of my parental responsibilities; thank you. She could learn a thing or two from me on that score. I'm always there for my super-talented daughter. She has the voice of an angel and could give Katherine Jenkins a run for her money. Have I told you she won a Scholarship for the University of Arts London?

PATRICK:
You have once or twice, yes.

Jim looks proud. He sits down oh his swivel chair in front of Patrick and picks up the photo of Lucy from his desk.

PATRICK: (CONT'D)

Another thing - Vanessa said your mother called her asking if you can buy her some new slippers and take them around tonight.

JIM:

Honestly? I don't even know why she needs new slippers. I don't think she's been out of bed for two years. (SIGHS) I'll buy a pair and drop them around on the way to see Lucy. Is that all?

PATRICK:

No. (PAUSES) Oh, she's fed up with telling you that the kitchen television's on the blink and if you don't get it fixed, she'll buy a new one, put it on your card and shove the old one straight up your...

JIM:

Bum?

PATRICK:

She said 'arse' but as least you know where it will be going.

JIM:

How very quaint. I'll get someone to go over there later in the week. I'm telling you, she's made me a broken man, Patrick. Look what that woman's turned me into. I'm a...

PATRICK:

Broken man? Yes, you keep saying.

JIM:

Are you suggesting that I repeat myself a lot?

PATRICK:

You do tend to.

EPISODE 2 - MAD WORLD

JIM:
(WITHOUT SARCASM) Really? I repeat myself a lot?

Jim opens a drawer in his desk. He takes out a packet of chocolate digestives and takes one out and starts eating it.

JIM: (CONT'D)
Heaven knows why the boyfriend can't do that himself. I bet the plug has a blown fuse. That's all.

PATRICK:
And don't forget, Natalie starts today. She'll be here shortly.

Patrick points at his watch, but Jim is engrossed in the ingredients on the biscuit packet.

JIM:
Hmmm. Natural flavourings? Are all the rest of the flavours in these biccies, *unnatural* then? Are they, in fact, an affront to Mother Nature herself?

PATRICK:
The new girl? Remember, you hired her last week? You've become very easily distracted and forgetful in your old age.

JIM:
Oh blimey, I clean forgot. Do I look alright? Do we have enough tea, coffee and sugar? Is the health and safety instruction poster back on the wall? Oh, and make sure the toilet's clean.

Jim pushes another biscuit in his mouth and replaces the packet in the drawer. He frantically brushes himself down, then tidies his desk.

PATRICK:

You didn't worry about all of that when I started here. I don't think we had any bog paper for two weeks.

JIM:

Yes, well, you're different.

PATRICK:

What do you mean 'different'?

JIM:

Well, don't take it personally, boy, but, you're an animal.

PATRICK:

Oh, cheers, boss. You know, I could get very hurt by that.

JIM:

Right, I'm just popping out to get some provisions before we open.
When Natalie turns up, tell her I'm in an important meeting with the company accountant, and I'll be back presently.

Jim grabs his coat, checks himself in the mirror, runs his fingers through his hair and leaves the shop by the back door.

FADE TO:

EPISODE 2 - MAD WORLD

ACT 1, SCENE 3. INT. PAWN SHOP, BEHIND COUNTER [9.30 AM]

SHOT OF WALL CLOCK BEHIND THE COUNTER. IT SHOWS 9.30.

Patrick is serving a witless CUSTOMER and presents him with a pawn contract to sign.

PATRICK:
Could you just sign there please on all three copies... on the dotted line... in the box... where it says signature... where I'm pointing with my pen... repeatedly.

CUSTOMER #1:
Oh, you want me to sign there?

PATRICK:
If it's not too much trouble for you.

CUSTOMER #1:
No need for the attitude, son.

PATRICK:
(UNDER HIS BREATH) If I were your son, mate, I would have had myself adopted.

Patrick pulls the three signed contract pages and hands back the customer's copy.

PATRICK: (CONT'D)
Thank you so much, sir.

He counts the money out.

> PATRICK: (CONT'D)
> And here's your £50—ten, twenty, thirty, forty, fifty of your finest British pounds. And a good day to you, sir.

The customer folds his contract and puts it with the cash into his trouser pocket. He walks out, passing Jim who is carrying two shopping bags. Jim makes his way to the office and dumps the shopping on his desk.

> JIM:
> Why do women always have to wait until after they have packed their shopping away before getting their purses out? Then they cluelessly paw through it before realising they didn't have enough cash in the first place.

Then it's the same malarkey searching for a debit card. And once again with the reward card - that's been left it at home too.

> PATRICK:
> All women?

> JIM:
> Yes, I'd say so.

> PATRICK:
> It's that sort of wild generalisation that makes you such a hit with the ladies, Jim.

> NATALIE:
> (FROM THE KITCHEN) Excuse me, but we're not all like that, you know.

Into the office walks an attractive, slim woman in her mid-thirties holding a mug of tea. She hands it to Patrick.

JIM:
Oh, hello, Natalie. I didn't know you were here yet. I was just…

Natalie glances at the two bags.

NATALIE:
In a meeting with your accountant. Yes, Patrick explained.

Natalie's phone rings from her handbag in the kitchen. She lets it continue to ring.

JIM:
Aren't you going to answer that?

NATALIE:
No. It's just my ex-boyfriend begging me to take him back.

There is an awkward moment as the phone continues to ring. Finally, it stops. Jim breaks the silence.

JIM:
So, on the way back, I just nipped to the supermarket to get some bits and pieces that young Patrick forgot to buy. If you wouldn't mind putting the shopping away, please, Patrick?

Patrick raises his eyebrows to Natalie, who smiles back at him. He picks up the shopping and disappears into the kitchen. The shop door opens. A young man approaches the counter. He drops a watch into the drawer under the counter.

JIM: (CONT'D)
(TO NATALIE) Well, there's no time like the present to get you started. Come with me and watch and learn… watch and learn.

CUSTOMER #2:
How much will you give me to pawn my 'Rolex,' mate?

JIM:
Your 'Rolex'? Now, let me see… Hmmm, now I can immediately see that there are a couple of slight issues with this. And when I say 'a couple of slight issues', what I really mean is that there are about half a dozen huge problems.

CUSTOMER #2:
What do you mean? My girlfriend… I mean, my Mum bought it for me as a present.

JIM:
(ASIDE TO NATALIE) Unusual family set up.(TO CUSTOMER) Just by looking and feeling this, err, piece, I can ascertain that it's not quite the real McCoy. You see, there are a few things we look at before we can ascertain if a watch is the genuine article. Your timepiece, if indeed it does tell the time… ain't real.

Jim glances at Natalie and winks.

JIM:(CONT'D.)
Firstly, it weighs less than an ant's appendix. Secondly, the gold-coloured plating is flaking off in my hands. Thirdly, the 'R' in Rolex on the face looks like it wants no partof this charade, and is making a run for it. Fourthly, the date window has dropped off. See?

Jim holds up the watch in front of the customer. Natalie looks impressed. Jim is in his element.

JIM: (CONT.)
Fifthly, the bracelet clasp doesn't snap shut, and finally, and just as

expected, the thing is not even working.

CUSTOMER #2:

Oh, I see. So how much exactly would you give me for it then?

JIM:

Nothing, nowt, nicht, zilch, zip, bugger all. This is an ex-watch. It has ceased to exist. It's gone to meet...

The customer interrupts oblivious to Jim's Python reference.

CUSTOMER #2:

So, not even a tenner then?

NATALIE:

What my boss is telling you, sir is that unfortunately, we won't be able to lend you anything on your watch, but if you have anything else of value, we'd be more than happy to look at it for you and hopefully lend you some money.

CUSTOMER #2:

Oh, fair enough.

Jim gives the customer his watch back and he leaves the shop. Jim looks at Natalie and nods. He loved that Natalie referred to him as 'boss'.

JIM:

Nice one. I think we'll make a good team, you and I. You know what the customer wants to hear, don't you?

NATALIE:

I'd like to think so. I expect that's one of the reasons you hired me, isn't it?

JIM:
Yes, it's undoubtedly one of the reasons. I can tell you have much to offer. It's an interesting job, and you'll be servicing all sorts of customers – and I mean all sorts. I've done my best with Patrick, but he lacks finesse. He doesn't take much in, you see.

Out of nowhere, a booming female voice hollers.

VANESSA: (O.O.V)
Patrick lacks finesse? That's rich coming from you, James.

Jim's ex-wife, Vanessa is standing at the front door. She strides up to the counter. Her hair is beautifully coiffured and is wearing a long, expensive looking coat and high heels. Jim stands to attention. Vanessa pays Natalie a cursory glance before dropping a Shoe Zone bag into the counter drawer.

VANESSA: (CONT'D)
Don't take too much notice of this one, sweetheart; he's a terrible flirt. And please don't ever ask him to mend a leaky tap or come round to fix your faulty television as he'll never get round to it.

Anyway, James, this is for your mother. I assumed you'd forget or not even bother, even after my call, so I bought them myself.

You're lucky I'm still quite fond of your Mum. By the way, the address of the concert hall for Lucy's performance is on an envelope in the bag. I can also assume you've forgotten that too. Lucy knows I've got a Reiki session and I've already apologise so there's no need to labour that point to her. Anyway, I must be off; I have a hair appointment. And once again...

JIM:
(INTERRUPTS) By the way, this is Natalie. She started with us today.

NATALIE:
Hello, Mrs Trueman. I'm pleased to meet you.

VANESSA:
(DISMISSIVELY) Yes, hello, dear. (TURNING TO JIM) James, you know how important getting the tax return finished is – I don't want to receive a second threatening reminder from HMRC.

With a swish of her coat, Vanessa turns and exits the shop.

JIM:
So now you've met, or should I say 'witnessed' my ex-wife and, unfortunately, current business partner. Only she and my mother call me James. Neither of them like me very much.

NATALIE:
She seems quite… high maintenance. Very demanding.

JIM:
You could say that. She makes Mariah Carey appear like…

Jim pauses in thought.

NATALIE:
Keanu Reeves?

JIM:
Yes, so they say! We appear to be on the same wavelength. Anyway, Vanessa and I have been divorced for three years now. It was relatively amicable, and we both got what we wanted from the split. - she got the house, the car and half of the business and I got the school fees, the mortgage payments and three and a half pairs of my shoes that she hadn't already

chucked in a skip. (SIGHS)She left me a broken man, Natalie.

NATALIE:

So I've heard. If I may say, I didn't like the way she spoke to you. Have you ever thought of killing her?

JIM:

What?

NATALIE:

Joke. It was just a joke.

JIM:

Oh right. Yes, a joke.

Jim walks back into the office.

JIM: (O.O.V) (CONT'D)

…and yes, I have. Frequently and in great detail. That was a joke too, by the way.

END OF ACT 1

ACT 2

ACT 2, SCENE 1 PAWN OFFICE – [11.15 AM]

SHOT OF NATALIE'S PHONE. IT SHOWS 11.15 AM

Natalie sits opposite Jim and sneaks a peek at the messages on her

EPISODE 2 - MAD WORLD

phone as Jim is pre-occupied with the tax return. Patrick is counting the pledges in the safe. A wild-haired, beaming octogenarian, MRS MULLANEY, shuffles into the shop.

MRS MULLANEY:
Cooey, Jimmy! Are you there? Is anyone there?

JIM:
Oh for Pete's sake. (THROWS DOWN PEN IN FRUSTRATION) It's not like I had anything to do today. Hello Mrs Mullaney! (TO NATALIE) Shadow me.

Jim enters the shop. Natalie stands in the doorway.

JIM: (CONT'D)
How are you today?

MRS MULLANEY:
Oh, I'm good, thanks. I've been busy cooking you something.

JIM:
Oh, joy.

Mrs Mullaney presents a Tupperware box full of a brown sludge. She places it in the drawer under the counter. Jim looks at it in trepidation before carefully lifting it out as if it is an unexploded bomb.

JIM: (CONT'D)
Oh wow, Elaine, this is… is… Actually, what is it?

MRS MULLANEY:
It's my special chicken curry, Jimmy. Special, because I made it for my two special boys. Oh, and who's this?

Mrs Mullaney notices Natalie who is staring at her phone again.

JIM

This is Natalie. She's just started with us.

MRS MULLANEY

Hello dear. Come closer. I won't bite.

PATRICK:

Natalie, this is Mrs Mullaney. (ASIDE) Mrs Elaine E. Mullaney. You couldn't make it up.

NATALIE:

Hello, Mrs Mullaney.

MRS MULLANEY:

I've known Jimmy and Patrick for years. They can get very busy, particularly around lunchtime, and I hate to think of them working a whole day on an empty stomach, so when I'm coming up to town, I'll often cook them something and bring it in.

JIM:

That's right. Elaine often brings us in… little treats. Every few days, another little treat. We're special boys, alright.

MRS MULLANEY:

And now, you can have some too, dear. Anyway, this was just a flying visit. I've got to pop to the post office. I need to buy a postal order to send to my grandson in New Zealand – it's his birthday next week. Then I've got an appointment with the chiropodist.

I'm a martyr to my feet, you know. Anyway, it was nice meeting you, Natasha. Ta-ra. I hope you like it. It's a little bit hot, but my boys like things a bitspicy.

EPISODE 2 - MAD WORLD

Mrs Mullaney leaves the shop, leaving Jim and Natalie staring at the Tupperware box. Jim is unable to take his eyes off the curry.

JIM:
Do postal orders even exist anymore - and if they do, is it even currency in New Zealand?

Patrick appears on the scene. The curry pulls him in like a tractor beam.

PATRICK:
Is it me, or did that box just move?

JIM:
You timed that well. It's Mrs Mullaney's latest attempt to kill us. Patrick, carefully, very carefully, pick it up and slowly take it into the office.

Patrick does as he is told. He places the box on Jim's desk. Jim and Natalie follow him. Patricks prods the box with a pencil.

JIM: (CONT'D)
Careful! Don't anger it.

PATRICK:
If this is as bowel-bashingly damaging as her recent chilli con *carnage* then I, for one, don't want any part of it.

NATALIE:
Surely, it can't be that potent?

JIM:
Don't you believe it. That brown hell is housed in no ordinary Tupper-

ware. It has an invisible layer of asbestos, I'm telling you. It's burning my eyes by just by looking at it.

Natalie laughs.

JIM: (CONT'D)
Patrick, you know the drill. Take it out the back and destroy it in a controlled explosion, would you?

PATRICK:
Why me?

JIM:
Because you're expendable. Just do as you're told, lad.

Patrick picks up the box again and stands rigid.

NATALIE:
What will he do with it?

JIM:
He'll flush the incendiary material down the toilet and dispose of the box, in not one, but two flimsy Poundland carrier bags. He'll then dispose of it off the premises in the street bin out front. It's the only sensible thing to do.

NATALIE:
Poor old Mrs Mullaney.

JIM:
You say 'poor' Mrs Mullaney, but I'm sure she's trying to kill us with her experimental cooking. I'm telling you, that stuff was pure napalm. If she cooked that on Masterchef, Greg Wallace would react - "It's like angels kissing my tongue. Hold on; it's more like devils piercing it with pitchforks.

Like a deadly assassin, the heat is coming throughit. Hang on. Oh, bloody hell. What the f…" before spontaneously combusting.

She made a chocolate bombe for us a few weeks ago. The 'oozing' centre was denser than a neutron star. It certainly wasn't full of what he'd call "gooey loveliness."

(TO PATRICK) Come on, lad, Get going. Do your duty for the sake of Queen and country. Oh, you might want to wear a pair of these.

Jim throws Patrick a box of latex gloves which bounce off his chest and fall to the ground.

JIM: (CONT'D)

If anything happens, I'll make sure your remains are delivered to your mother. And I'll write a beautiful obituary for the local paper. It's the least I can do.

PATRICK:

You're all heart. (MUMBLES)This is not in my job description, you know?

Natalie stifles a giggle.

NATALIE:

You're so cruel to him.

JIM:

I know. Good, isn't it? I suppose I'd better get on with this tax return before the next reminder from the old hag.

FADE TO:

ACT 2, SCENE 2. EXT. PAWN SHOP, [12 PM]

SHOT OF THE TOWN HALL CLOCKFACE. IT'S BELLS PEEL FOR 12 PM.

Patrick is wiping over the countertops is alerted to GEORGE, the window cleaner as he slaps his soapy rag onto the window outside. Patrick approaches him.

PATRICK:
And what time do you call this?

GEORGE:
Now listen here, young man. I'm usually doing your windows early in the morning while you're still dragging your sad carcass down the road from the station. The reason I've been delayed is I've been cleaning the windows of a new and rather influential client.

PATRICK:
Alright, alright, I was only kidding. So, who is this mysterious new client?

GEORGE:
I'm not at liberty to say. One has to treat one's client list as totally confidential.
If any of my competitors were to find out, it could cause mayhem; absolute mayhem.

PATRICK:
Mayhem? I didn't realise. Very well, I won't enquire further.

George beckons Patrick towards him.

GEORGE:
Okay, I'll tell you, but it goes no further. Understand?

PATRICK:
Your secret is safe with me.

GEORGE:
It better be.(MAKING SURE NO-ONE IS LISTENING) You know that Piers Morgan?

PATRICK:
Really? You do his windows?

GEORGE:
No, no, I can only dream of cleaning the stained glass and leaded lights of his palatial pad. No, it's the woman who does his make-up on GMTV.

PATRICK:
Wow, George, that's… impressive. I think.

GEORGE:
You don't need to tell me that. Anyway, you make sure you keep it under your hat. Oh, and I understand you've got a new girl starting today.

PATRICK:
Yes, Natalie. She's lovely. (PAUSES) Hold on, how did you know about her?

George taps the side of his nose.

GEORGE:
I'm not at liberty to divulge that information. A secret told to a window cleaner is a secret kept.

PATRICK:

So, it was Jim, then?

GEORGE:

(PAUSES) Yes. I saw him coming out of the Poundland earlier on. Right, I can't stand around talking to you all day. I have work to do, as I'm sure you do too.

PATRICK:

You're absolutely right. I best get on. And George…

GEORGE:

What?

Patrick emulates George, tapping the side of his nose.

PATRICK:

Your secret is safe with me.

FADE TO:

ACT 2, SCENE 3. OUTSIDE THE FRONT OF THE SHOP [1.20PM]

SHOT OF NATALIE'S MOBILE PHONE. IT'S 1.20 PM

Natalie goes through the text messages on her phone. There are half a dozen messages, all from her ex-boyfriend, Kit and are all very apologetic; asking her to forgive him. She quickly texts a reply.

I'm sorry, Kit, but I've moved on. I suggest you do too. I've said all there needs to be said.

She puts the phone back into her bag and walks away down the street.

FADE TO:

ACT 2, SCENE 4. INT. OFFICE [1.30 PM]

A RADIO IS ON AT LOW VOLUME IN THE BACKGROUND. A NEWSCASTER ANNOUNCES IT'S 1.30 PM

Jim and Patrick are sitting, eating lunch. Jim has a prawn sandwich and Patrick, a bag of chips. He's a messy eater and has dropped a few on the floor.

PATRICK:

I spoke to old George this morning. He said he bumped into you earlier on.

JIM:

Oh yes. I imagine he told you about Piers Morgan's make-up artist, and that he told you not to tell anyone? However, he told me, the road-sweeper and a random old woman outside Poundland and who knows who else. Honestly, who does he think would find that remotely interesting, let alone run to the national press with the scoop of the century?

PATRICK:

(STUDYING HIS CHIPS) I don't know. Oh, and he knew about Natalie too.

JIM:

Yes, he was quite enthralled. He tapped his nose and assured me my secret as safe with him. Quite bizarre. (PAUSES) So, what do you think?

PATRICK:

Yeah, not bad, but I don't think they're half as good as the ones from the old chippie next to the station. Now they did great chips. It's all about the oil they're cooked in.

JIM:

No, I don't mean your bloody chips, you idiot - I'm talking about our new girl. I'm talking about Natalie.

PATRICK:

Oh right. Yes, I like her, and actually, I think she quite likes me too.

JIM:

I don't think so, mate. Not in the way you think. Did you see how she was shadowing me all morning? I think she appreciates the older gentleman – a father figure, perhaps.

PATRICK:

Father figure? More like a Grandfather figure. And besides, she was shadowing you, because you instructed her to, by saying, "Shadow me. Watch and learn." I mean, "watch and learn" – How patronising do you want to be? Besides, she was giving me the eye earlier on.

JIM:

She gave you 'the eye' because you sprayed half a can of Sprite down all over you when you opened it. You honestly do have the finesse of…

(DESPERATLEY TRYING TO THINK OF AN ANALOGY) of… of an inebriated yak on heat.

Jim looks very proud of himself.

PATRICK:

'To live means to finesse the processes to which one is subjugated.'

JIM:

What?? Where the hell did you get that from? Don't tell me it's from one of your heroes. Now was it Rylan Clarke-Neal? Kylie Jenner? Or could it possibly have been the fragrant Miss Gemma Collins?

PATRICK:

Actually, Jim, the quote is attributed to Bertold Brecht.

JIM:

(SHOCKED) How the hell do you know that?

PATRICK:

I read it on a poster in the tube station last week.

JIM:

And do you even know who Bertold Brecht was? You probably think he played for Borussia Mönchengladbach in the 1970s - a silky and skilful central midfielder with an ability to make pinpoint cross-field passes and with a penchant for fine French wines, Italian designer shoes, and the odd pithy comment.

PATRICK:

So, who did he play for then?

JIM:

Bayern Munich, of course. I thought everybody knew that.

Jim shakes his head despairingly.

JIM: (CONT'D)

Come on, let's clear this mess up; we don't want Natalie to come back from lunch, thinking we like living in a pigsty – although you can only aspire to such decadence. Leave me in peace now as I need to get this bloody tax return finished. I'm in the home straight now. Look at that. All neat and perfectly legible. Why would I need to do it online?

Patrick flicks 'V's behind Jim's back.

END OF ACT 2

EPISODE 2 - MAD WORLD

ACT 3

ACT 3, SCENE 1. INT. PAWN SHOP. [4.00 PM]

SHOT OF BOTTOM OF COMPUTER SCREEN. IT SHOWS 4 PM

Jim's phone rings. He turns his back to Natalie and answers the call.

JIM:
(WHISPERING AGITATEDLY) Yes, Vanessa, I haven't forgotten. I'm doing it now. I am. I promise you. No, I'm not lying to you...

Still on the phone, Jim walks away to the back door and storms out of the building. Patrick comes into the shop and leans on the back wall next to Natalie.

NATALIE:
Basil and Sybil.

PATRICK:
Sorry?

NATALIE:
Basil and Sybil Fawlty. Fawlty Towers?

PATRICK:
Oh yes. I see what you mean. Then that makes me Manuel. (IN A TERRIBLE SPANISH ACCENT) *I know nuuthiiing.*

NATALIE:
So I've been told.

PATRICK:
You what?

NATALIE:
I was just kidding. I'm sure you know plenty.

Patrick ponders the flirtatious comment, but his train of thought is broken as Jim re-enters, mumbling loudly. He sits down at the desk and takes out his packet of biscuits. Natalie and Patrick join him.

JIM:

She doesn't know when to quit, that woman. Not satisfied with taking my house, and half of my business, she's now cost me £400 for a new kitchen television. She realised I'm 'not capable of fixing it', so she's only gone and ordered a new one and with 'same-day delivery' if you please. It bet it wasn't playing up in the first place – just not quite the right shade of ecru to match her new fitted cabinets. You know something – she's left me…

PATRICK & NATALIE:

(IN UNISON) A broken man?

JIM:

Yes, that's right—a broken man. You know, I wouldn't mind, well I would mind, but she never watches much TV, unless it's The Real Housewives of Beverley Hills. Oh, she'd love to star in The Real Housewives of Winchmore Hill, where she could slag me off at every opportunity to her coven of witches. Damn woman!

PATRICK:

Calm down, Jim, you'll give yourself a connery.

JIM:

A what?

PATRICK:

A connery. You know, like a heart attack. You need to relax. Have another biscuit.

JIM:

First of all, Patrick, it's a coronary, and secondly, a chocolate digestive is

EPISODE 2 - MAD WORLD

not going to calm me down or get that she-devil off my back.

PATRICK:
Okay, okay. I was just trying to help.

Natalie shields her face, trying not to laugh at Patrick's malapropism.

NATALIE:
Look, I'll put the kettle on and make us all a nice cup of tea.

PATRICK:
I don't think tea will solve his problems either, Natalie.

JIM:
Oh, shut up, Patrick. (TO NATALIE) Thank you, Natalie, that will be lovely. I'm sure it will help.

NATALIE: (O.S.)
One sugar. Stirred, not shaken?

JIM:
(Impersonates Sean Connery) Exshelent. Thatsh jusht the way I like it, Miss Moneypenny.

PATRICK:
'He pulls a knife, you pull a gun. He sends one of yours to the hospital, you send one of his to the morgue'.

Natalie pokes her head around the kitchen door and both she and Jim stare at Patrick.

PATRICK: (CONT'D)
It's from The Untouchables. I thought we were doing Sean Coronary

impressions.

Jim shakes his head in disbelief.

FADE TO:

ACT 3, SCENE 2. INT. SHOP. [5.15 PM]

SHOT OF JIM'S WATCH. IT SHOWS 5.15

Just about to sign and date the tax return, Jim is alerted to a dishevelled, middle-aged man enter the shop. Patrick is preparing to take out the rubbish as it's refuse collecting night. An exasperated Jim stands up and with the papers in hand, walks over to the counter.

JIM:
Shadow me, Natalie.

Jim puts his papers down beside the printer and faces the customer.

MR JEFFRIES:
How much will you give me for this?

MR JEFFRIES drops a chain and a bracelet into the drawer.

JIM:
Do you want to pawn them or sell them?

MR JEFFRIES:
What's the difference?

JIM:
Well, if you pawn them, we will lend you an amount of money, and once you pay it back along with some interest, you can have them back. However, if you sell them, well, you sell them.

MR JEFFRIES:
I want to sell it.

JIM:
Okay then.

MR JEFFRIES:
But I might want to get it back.

JIM:
You can't. Only if you pawn them, can you get them back.

Jim gives Natalie a look of mock disbelief as the customer ponders his next move.

MR JEFFRIES:
Right, I think I'll probably pawn it then... but I might not come back.

NATALIE:
(TO JIM) Is this guy for real?

JIM:
(TO NATALIE) Welcome to my world. You have entered the Twilight Zone– where reality and fiction are forever intertwined.
(TO CUSTOMER) Do you have any ID on you?

MR JEFFRIES:
Yes, I've got a letter here.

JIM:
Good.

MR JEFFRIES:
But it's not mine; it's my brother-in-law's. He gets his post delivered to my house. His home was fire-bombed by kids.

JIM:
Of course. That's entirely reasonable. However, if it's not your name on it, it can't identify you; therefore, it's not ID, is it?

MR JEFFRIES:
I've pawned it before, though.

JIM:
Why didn't you say? What's your name?

MR JEFFRIES:
Jeffries. The name is Jeffries.
JIM:
And your first name?

MR JEFFRIES:
Jeff.

JIM:
(LOOKS AT NATALIE)Jeffrey Jeffries? Your middle name isn't Jeffrey, by chance, is it?

MR JEFFRIES:
(No, of course, that would be ridiculous.

JIM:
Yes, I suppose it would be. Well, I can't find any Jeff Jeffries on my system, sir.

MR JEFFRIES:
Oh, it wasn't here. It was a shop in Margate. I was on holiday there last year. Strange bloke - the fella who owned it. He was very offish towards me like he couldn't wait to get rid of me.

Jim and Natalie look at each other in incredulity.

MR JEFFRIES: (CONT'D)
Hold on a minute. I think I've got another letter with my name on it.

JIM:
Why didn't you give me that in the first place?

MR JEFFRIES:
You didn't ask. There you are. So, how much can you give me for it?

Jim takes a huge intake of breath and weighs the bracelet and chain.

JIM:
Just to confirm, there are two items here, sir: a chain and a bracelet. I can offer you £220 for the pair of them... *both* of them. *Both* the chain and the bracelet... £220 for *both* of your items.

MR JEFFRIES:
That's a fair price. It's only sitting in my bedside cabinet drawer.

Jim tries to keep calm as he enters the details into the computer. He prints out the contract and presents it to the customer to sign.

JIM:
There we go. Please sign in the box, by the cross.

MR JEFFRIES:
No, I don't want to do it now. I just wanted to know what you would give me if I pawned it, or sold it.

Jim slams the papers down on top of the tax return he left by the printer.

JIM:
Here, take your thingsss… your thingsssss; both of them and please leave my shop. You, sir, are a time-waster. Just go.

MR JEFFRIES:
You're a very rude man. Even ruder than the bloke in Margate, I'll take my chain and go somewhere else.

JIM:
(SHOUTING) That's it. Patrick! Patrick! Get the rubbish out and lock up. I've had enough today.
Besides, I need to go to see my decrepit old mother anyway before she goes to sleep at the ungodly late hour of 7 PM.

Jim's phone rings.

JIM (CONT'D)
Yes, I've done the tax return and I've got the bloody bag with the bloody slippers - and the address! Good luck at your oh-so-important Reiki session and do enjoy experiencing the cultural phenomenon of your Dreadful Housewives of Hades on my pristine, brand new, colour-coordinated television as you slave over the microwave for four and a half minutes while your delicious M&S Fettuccine Carbonara for two gets radiated for

you and your toy boy.

I'm surprised you didn't fleece me for a few extra quid for a couple of fillet steaks too. Anyway, I'll bid you adieu as I'll shortly off to visit your delightful ex-mother- in-law. Good day, Vanessa.

Jim ends the call.

JIM (CONT'D)

I'm pretty sure she ended the call as soon as I told her the tax returns were done, in truth. I'm sorry about this, Natalie. It's just the perfect end to a perfect day. I can assure you, not every day is as bad as this.

Jim rips up Mr Jeffries' contract unaware that the tax return was at the bottom of the pile and throws them in the bin. He returns to the office to cash up. Patrick brushes past Natalie with the rubbish sack and empties the bin into it.

PATRICK:

(TO NATALIE) And quite often, it's worse.

Natalie walks over to Jim who is putting the takings into the safe.

NATALIE:

It's okay, Jim, I've worked in retail before, and I know what a royal pain in the backside the general public can be; and as for your ex-wife, she is very similar to my stepmother. She's never satisfied, and deep down, she is probably a very sad and miserable person. (SHE PUTS HER HAND ON HIS SHOULDER). I can tell you're a good man, and that's very important in my book.

Jim stops in his tracks. Natalie's hand is still on his shoulder.

JIM:

Thank you, Natalie. That means a lot. It really does.

NATALIE:

Just take a deep breath and go and visit your Mum. I'm sure she'll be happy to see you.

JIM:

You don't know my mother. She took Vanessa's side when my marriage broke up. She also blames me for her being unable to walk without pain for more than four steps.

According to her, she caught osteoarthritis in her hips and back from lifting me into my pram as a baby. She genuinely believes that you know.

NATALIE:

Well, I don't know what to say. Perhaps she's...

JIM:

A sandwich short of a picnic? A playing card short of a full deck. Err... a bludgeon to the head with a blunt instrument short of a murder?

NATALIE:

I was going to say, a little confused. Look, I'm sure you have some good things in your life. Patrick tells me you have a very talented daughter.

JIM:

Ah, yes, thank goodness for my Lucy. She understands her old man.

NATALIE:

There you go. She loves you. (PAUSES AND LOOKS AROUND), and Jim,

I know we barely know each other, but I need to tell you that...

EPISODE 2 - MAD WORLD

JIM:
(IN EXCITED ANTICIPATION) Yes? Natalie - what is it?

NATALIE:
Jim, I need to tell you… that you have a huge mayonnaise smear on your tie. I've just noticed it.

JIM:
Oh no. It must have been there for ages. I had my lunch over four hours ago.

NATALIE:
Sorry, I just noticed it. Hold on, let me get a wet cloth, I'll get that off.

Natalie fetches a tea towel, wets it under the tap and returns. She dabs the stain on Jim's tie. She is very close to him and he can feel her breath on his face. Patrick re- appears. Jim looks smugly at him.

JIM:
You know, Natalie, you might be right. Things might not quite as bad as they might seem.

NATALIE:
They rarely are. You have been taken advantage of by a lot of people. I think you're great.

JIM:
That's some testimony, young lady. Quite often, I look in the mirror and think I must be mad to take all the crap I do.

NATALIE:
I didn't say you weren't mad. Besides, we're all a little mad, aren't It's only the insane who believe they're not mad.

Natalie gives Jim a little hug and a kiss on the cheek and walks into the kitchen. Patrick looks horrified.

JIM:
Proof if proof were ever needed, mate.

Jim tries to find the tax return. He suddenly remembers where he left it and as soon as he gets to the printer, he realises what he's done.

JIM: (CONT'D)
Oh God. Patrick! Patrick!

PATRICK:
What's wrong?

JIM:
Did you throw away a ripped up contract I left beside the printer?

PATRICK:
Yes, don't worry, I put it in the rubbish sack.

Jim runs to the front door just in time to see the refuse collector throw the sack into the trash compactor before the truck drives away.

FADE TO:

ACT 3, SCENE 3. INT. CAR. [5.40 PM]

SHOT OF THE CAR CLOCK. IT SHOWS 5.45 PM

EPISODE 2 - MAD WORLD

Jim sits in his car. He waits with the windows down at the inevitable red light. He is singing along to 'Come Up And See (Make Me Smile)' and spies an elderly man on a roadside bench staring at him. He turns down the volume.

JIM:
It's okay, mate; It turns out, I may be a little mad.

The man continues staring at him.

JIM: (CONT'D)
Don't you believe me? I'm mad because my ex-wife hates me, but I've just spent £400 on a new television for her; mad because all day I've been carefully completing a tax return that I later accidentally destroyed, so I have to do the whole thing again online, thus proving that ex-wife right; mad because I'm deluding myself that a young lady who started working for me today, possibly has the hots for me; mad because even though my mother hates me, I'm leaving work early to run up to her nursing home, (which I pay for), to take her some new slippers that she won't even wear.

He then realises he's left them at work.

JIM: (CONT'D)
No, I won't be doing that because I've left the bloody things at work along with the address to my daughter's performance tonight and now I'm going to have to concedeto phone the hex and admit that I've lost the address; and mad because I'm singing to a total stranger from my car.

Jim begins to sing again

JIM: (CONT'D)
Come up and see me...make me smiiiiiile. Or do want you want, running wiiiiild. Now you think I'm mad too, yes?

The old man looks confused. The traffic lights turn green and Jim drives off.

JIM: (V.O.)

What a day! Along with the wicked witch of the West flying in with my mother's, not so ruby slippers and probably the biggest arse of a customer I have ever laid eyes on. And then there's Natalie – a beacon of light. So what if an attractive girl who's much too young takes a fancy to me? I might just have something to offer - something Vanessa couldn't see in me. Perhaps she'll be able to fix this broken man.

EXT.SHOT OF THE CAR DRIVING OFF DOWN A LEAFY SUBURBAN STREET.

END OF ACT AND EPISODE

Episode 3 - Electric Dreams

Written by Elliot Stanton

ACT ONE

ACT 1, SCENE 1. INT. JIM'S CAR [8.30 AM]

FADE IN:
SHOT OF CAR RADIO CLOCK. IT SHOWS 8.30 AM. JIM IS DRIVING TO WORK.

JIM has stopped at red traffic lights. He looks in the rearview mirror and straightens his eyebrows with his fingers.

JIM: (V.O.)
You've still got it, Jimbo. A second date, tonight. The lovely Kerry won't know what's hit her. Posh nosh and a bottle of chilled Champagne or two, coupled with the old Trueman charm - she'll be putty in your hands.

The radio news starts.

RADIO NEWS:
'Following the findings from an independent review, The Secretary of State for Energy has forced energy providers to place a price cap on how much they can charge customers for gas and electricity. From March next year, the consumer will save an estimated one billion pounds on household energy bills...

JIM:
About bloody time. Mind you, with the electricity I'll be creating tonight...

RADIO NEWS:
'However, according to many of the 'big six' suppliers, the price rises already

announced for this year will still go ahead.'

Jim turns off the radio. A male cyclist rides up beside him and witnesses his rant.

JIM:

(ADDRESSES THE RADIO) My electricity bill has doubled in the last three years. The profits they make off poor saps like me are scandalous. They'll still find a way increase their profit margins, and if they do, they can just -
(LOOKS TOWARDS A PASSING CYCLIST WHOSE A LITTLE TO CLOSE) Piss off!

Jim's loud expletive, inadvertently causes the shocked cyclist to fall off his bike. Jim undoes his seatbelt to attend to him, but the lights change. He gets a hoot from the motorist behind him and drives off. From the rearview mirror, Jim is relieved to see the cyclist get up and brush himself down.

FADE TO:

ACT 1. SCENE 2 INT. SHOP [8.40 AM]

SHOT OF WALL CLOCK. IT SHOWS 8.40.

The front door opens and alarm sounds. Jim enters the code and it is silenced. He walks through to the office and switches on the lights.

Immediately, the lights go out.

JIM:

Oh, that's all I need. Not another power cut. It's the third one this month.

He opens the cupboard to the fuse box to check for tripped fuses. There are none. He sits at his desk in the darkness and takes out a packet of biscuits from a drawer. Jim tries to turn on the radio, but realities it was on mains power.

GEORGE, the window cleaner, bangs on the front door holding his squeegee mop like he was presenting arms. Jim greets him.

GEORGE:

Trying to save on the old electric, are we?

JIM:

No, it's another power cut.

GEORGE:

How long has it been?

JIM:

Only a couple of minutes.

GEORGE:

That's nothing. In the 70s, when we had the three-day week, we'd be sitting around a candle, eating cold baked beans night after night.

JIM:

(BARELY INTERESTED) Really?

EPISODE 3 - ELECTRIC DREAMS

George rests his mop on the window.

GEORGE:

Yes, really. One minute, you'll be happily watching Crossroads and the next. Vooom. It all went dark. We had an electric cooker at the time. More fool us. Many's the time, my wife, gawd rest her soul, had a roast in the oven when the electric went off. Bloody Ted Heath! You'd have to go shopping by candlelight or gaslight. Well, not personally, but the wife did. How can you expect to see what you are buying when you can barely see where you're going?

Just then, the lights came back on and the radio springs into life.

JIM:

Ahh, and as if by magic. As fascinating as your story is, George, I must go and prepare to open. I'll see you tomorrow.

Jim leaves George standing and locks the front door before walking back into the office. He halts at the safe. The display is flashing '00.00'

JIM: (CONT'D)

That's not right. Please don't tell me that's what I think that means.

Jim taps in the passcode. It beeps twice to indicate a problem. He tries again, to no avail. PATRICK, the shop assistant (22) knocks on the front door. Jim lets him in.

PATRICK:

Good morning, boss.

JIM:

No, Patrick, it isn't. It really isn't.

Jim leaves Patrick to lock the door and tries to open the safe again. He gets the same result.

PATRICK:

Is it jammed?

JIM:

No, we had another power cut. It lasted a bit longer than last time and the clock on the safe has reset, so it's time-locked.

PATRICK:

Can't you just re-set the time, yourself?

JIM:

Have you been on the stupid pills, lad? That would be an excellent security feature, wouldn't it- any old Tom, Dick or Harry being able to alter the time on the safe?

Presumably, you think it would be a good idea to leave a post-it note with the entry code on the door too? Right, the time, according to the display, is now one minute past midnight, so if all goes well, I will able to open the safe door in…oooh… just over eight bloody hours!

PATRICK:

But, we'll be shut by then.

An exasperated Jim takes sighs and stares at Patrick.

JIM:

You reckon, do you? I need to call Mr Jaffar, the safe engineer.

Jim searches for his number on his phone and calls him.

EPISODE 3 - ELECTRIC DREAMS

JIM: (CONT'D)

Mr Jaffar? It's Jim Trueman from Trueman's Pawnbrokers. We've got a problem... No, it's not stuck, again. The timer is faulty, so I can't open the safe... I know it's not supposed to do that. Anyway, can you come along to fix it?

...Well, as soon as you can. I need to open the shop, you see... Okay, I'll see you within the hour? Okay, in just *over* an hour then. Bye- bye.

PATRICK:

Is he coming, then?

JIM:

You heard me say, 'I'll see you in just over an hour', yes?

PATRICK:

Oh, yes.

Jim looks at Patrick in disbelief. There's another knock at the front door. It's NATALIE, the other assistant. Patrick opens the door.

NATALIE:

Good morning.

PATRICK:

It was, but we've had another power cut and the safe won't open. He's in a right mood.

NATALIE:

Great. That's just what I need.

Natalie and Patrick walk into the office.

NATALIE: (CONT'D)

Good morning, Jim.

JIM:

The safe won't open.

NATALIE:

(MOCKING) Good morning, Natalie, How are you? I'm fine, thanks. How about you?

JIM:

Sorry. If we can't open the safe, we can't open the shop. You know, I was actually in a good mood earlier. As soon as I get to work, it all goes wrong.

NATALIE:

Oh yes, you've got a date tonight, haven't you?

Jim doesn't hear Natalie's question.

JIM:

It's almost as if this shop is cursed.

PATRICK:

Maybe your ex-wife has put a curse on this building and anyone who works in it.
Patrick laughs and goes into the kitchen.

JIM:

I think you might be right.

Patrick pokes his head around the door.

PATRICK:

I was just kidding, Jim.

EPISODE 3 - ELECTRIC DREAMS

JIM:

It's just the sort of the that the old hex would do. She's determined to destroy me and leave me a broken man.

NATALIE:

I thought she's already left you a broken man.

JIM:

She has. But she'll make sure that I'll remain this way.

There is an uneasy peace until Patrick breaks the silence.

PATRICK:

Tea, anyone?

NATALIE:

Yes, please.

Patrick disappears into the kitchen again.

JIM:

I'll have a coffee. Black.

PATRICK: (O.S.)

Like your mood.

JIM:

Yes, just like my mood and you'll do well to remember that, my boy. Typical. On the rare occasion that I need to leave on time; this happens. He better be able to fix it, or I will not be happy.

PATRICK: (O.S.)

Like you're a perfect delight right now.

JIM:

One more wisecrack out of you. Just one more…

FADE TO:

ACT 1, SCENE 3. INT SHOP, BEHIND COUNTER [9.30 AM]

SHOT OF TIME ON COMPUTER SCREEN. IT SHOWS 9.30.

Jim and Natalie are playing chess on the counter.

JIM:

And I believe that is…check and mate.

NATALIE:

You're good at this.

JIM:

I was in the chess team at school.

NATALIE:

Impressive.

Jim looks pleased with himself.

PATRICK:

How come you've got a chess set here?

EPISODE 3 - ELECTRIC DREAMS

JIM:

One of my old employees was a player and in the days before computers and mobile phones, we used to play a bit when it was quiet. I should warn you that I've never lost to an employee.

PATRICK:

I'll give you a game.

JIM:

Oh, Patrick. I think that snakes and ladders might be more your scene.

PATRICK:

No, I can play. My Uncle taught me. Mind you, I haven't played for quite a while.

Jim looks at his watch.

JIM:

Go on, then. I guess we have a couple of minutes before Mr Jaffar arrives.

Jim and Patrick start their game and within a few moves, Jim is in trouble; after three more moves apiece, Patrick moves in for the kill.

PATRICK:

Checkmate.

Jim looks stunned.

JIM:

How on earth did you do that?

PATRICK:

Fancy another game?

There's a knock at the door.

JIM:

Ah, that'll be the safe engineer.

NATALIE:

Not unless he works for Royal Mail, it's not.

Jim opens the front door and signs for a parcel from a uniformed postal worker. He brings it back to the counter.

JIM:

'Miss Natalie Reyes.' Something you've ordered?

NATALIE:

I haven't ordered anything. What it can be?

PATRICK:

Go on, open it.

Natalie tears off the wrapping. She looks disappointed.

NATALIE:

A pancake maker? He thinks he can win me back with a pancake maker?

JIM:

He's still trying then?

PATRICK:

So you're not seeing him anymore then?

Patrick is ignored.

EPISODE 3 - ELECTRIC DREAMS

NATALIE:
Well, that's going straight in the bin.

PATRICK:
Hold on. Do you really not want it?

NATALIE:
No, I do not.

PATRICK:
Can I have it?

NATALIE:
If you want it - take it.

PATRICK:
Great.

Patrick takes the box away.

PATRICK:
That's my parents' anniversary present sorted then.

Jim checks his watch again.

JIM:
Right, it's been an hour.

He calls Mr Jaffar again.

JIM: (CONT'D)
(ON PHONE) Hello, Mr Jaffar. Jim Trueman, here. Yes, I know you said about an hour, but I can't open the shop unless I can get that safe open… Right, I'll see you soon.

JIM: (CONT'D)

Half an hour, he reckons.

PATRICK:

(SINGS) *Have a little patience, yeah. 'Cause the scars run so deep. It's been hard, but I have to believe.*

JIM:

What the hell is that supposed to mean?

PATRICK:

I don't really know. It's from a song by Take That.

JIM:

Is it?

PATRICK:

Yep. Patience. You need a bit of that.

JIM:

Patrick?

PATRICK:

What?

JIM:

Shut up.

FADE OUT:

END OF ACT ONE

ACT TWO

ACT 2, SCENE 1. EXT. SHOP [10.30 AM]
FADE IN:
SHOT OF TIME ON NATALIE'S PHONE. IT SHOWS 10.30.

Natalie is leaning against the wall, beside the shop and is on speakerphone to her ex-boyfriend, KIT.

NATALIE:

What will it take to get through to you, Kit?

KIT: (O.S.)

I just want to say 'sorry'.

NATALIE:

You've said sorry. You've said sorry a thousand times and I forgive you, but I don't want to be with you anymore.

KIT: (O.S.)

But, I've changed.

NATALIE:

Not that old line? I don't think you have - not if you believe that a lousy pancake maker will win me over.

KIT: (O.S.)

But, Natalie…

NATALIE:

I have to go. I'm at work.

Natalie ends the call and re-enters the shop. Jim is on the phone again to the safe engineer.

JIM:

But you said that an hour ago. Pardon? Your washing machine has broken and flooded your kitchen now? No, I don't disbelieve you… So, if you're lucky, you'll be here…soon. I'm sure you'll be lucky. I'll see you soon, then.

Jim puts the phone down.

NATALIE:

'I don't disbelieve you.' Nice use of the double negative, there.

JIM:

Did you hear that? 'My washing machine's broken and the kitchen is flooded'. What sort of idiot would believe a line like that? That's like saying, 'the dog ate my homework.' What a pathetic excuse.

PATRICK:

Or 'I left my sister on the bus.'

NATALIE:

What?

PATRICK:

That happened to me on the way home from school one day. It was on the

EPISODE 3 - ELECTRIC DREAMS

219 from Tooting Broadway to Clapham Junction.

JIM:
But you don't live anywhere near Clapham Junction.

PATRICK:
Exactly. I was lost. I guess the confusion muddled my mind and I forgot about my little sister.

JIM:
Patrick, I don't know where to start, so I won't. Who wants another game of chess?

PATRICK:
I will.

JIM:
Not you! Natalie?

Just then, there's another knock on the door.

JIM: (CONT'D)
At last.

MRS MULLANEY, a customer, is standing outside the shop holding something in a plastic bag.

MRS MULLANEY:
Cooey, Jimmy. It's me.

JIM:
Oh, for fu...

PATRICK:

(SHOUTING) One minute, Mrs Mullaney, I'll let you in.

Patrick unlocks the front door and lets Mrs Mullaney in. She toddles in and rests on the counter, slightly out of breath.

JIM:

Hello Elaine.

MRS MULLANEY:

Why aren't you open? It's not stocktaking day, is it?

JIM:

No, we've got a problem with the safe, but the engineer will be here any minute. In fact, if you'll excuse me, I'm just going to call him again to find out where he is.

Jim walks away into the office and Natalie comes out to greet Mrs Mullaney.

NATALIE:

Hello, Mrs Mullaney

MRS MULLANEY:

Hello…

NATALIE:

Natalie

MRS MULLANEY:

Oh yes. How are you enjoying working here?

NATALIE:

It's not too bad.

MRS MULLANEY:

Really? You look sad.

NATALIE:

Do I?

MRS MULLANEY:

Yes. I can always tell.

NATALIE:

I've just been having a bit of trouble with a bloke.

MRS MULLANEY:

Have you? Are you trying to keep him happy? The second best way to a man's heart is through his stomach. You know the best way, don't you? Take it from someone who knows, Natasha.

NATALIE:

Natalie. Actually, I'm trying to get rid of him, but he's not taking the hint.

MRS MULLANEY:

I see. I had that problem myself once. I had a little affair, you see. He was running a Latin dance class. I started going with my late husband, but he gave up after a couple of weeks - no stamina. I still wanted to learn and to my joy, I was paired up with Enrico, the teacher. He was in his mid-30s and let's say, I was old enough to be his mother; and not a young mother either. Ooh, he was gorgeous - gorgeous, young, fit and very active, if you know what I mean? When the lessons ended, it was me who became the teacher. I used those salsa moves on him alright.

NATALIE:
(LAUGHING) Oh, Mrs Mullaney, you dark horse, you.

MRS MULLANEY:
Anyway, my husband started asking questions - particularly when he found out the term had finished.

NATALIE:
Oh dear. What did he say?

MRS MULLANEY:
Not a lot. He was head of history at the local comprehensive school and he was having it away with the head of girl's P.E. Anyway, my relationship with Enrico was doomed.

NATALIE:
Was he married too?

MRS MULLANEY:
No, He couldn't keep up with me, so I joined a still life art class and copped off with one of the male models.

Natalie bursts into laughter. Meanwhile, Jim makes a call from the office.

JIM: (O.S.)
Answer your bloody phone, man.

MRS MULLANEY:
Anyway, I best not hang around today. Jimmy's not in a very good mood, is he? I'll leave these for you all. I made some chilli chicken slices.

Mrs Mullaney takes out a Tupperware box from her shopping bag and slips it in the drawer under the counter.

MRS MULLANEY: (CONT'D)

Can I just give you a little advice, Natasha?

NATALIE:

Natalie.

MRS MULLANEY:

Don't cut off your nose to spite your face. You may never get your looks back.

A perplexed Natalie lets Mrs Mullaney out. She re-joins Patrick and Jim in the office, who have just started another game of chess. She places the box of food down on a filing cabinet.

PATRICK:

Check!

JIM:

You're not going to beat me that easily, my son.

Jim moves his King, allowing Patrick to check mate it with his Queen.

PATRICK:

Check mate. In nine moves. Unlucky, champ.

JIM:

What the hell? How did you *do* that?

PATRICK:

Beginner's luck, I guess. Luck and a bit of skill.

There's a knock at the door. Standing outside is MR JAFFAR, the safe engineer.

JIM:

At last; and don't get cocky, Patrick. It doesn't suit you.

Jim leaves his desk to let him in.

NATALIE:

How come you're so good at chess? And don't give me that 'beginner's luck' rubbish.

PATRICK:

I've been playing since I was six. I started playing for my county, aged 11. Don't tell Jim though.

NATALIE:

You're terrible.

PATRICK:

He deserves it. All that 'I've never lost' bravado.

Jim re-appears with Mr Jaffar in tow.

JIM:

There it is, on the back wall.

MR JAFFAR:

Thank you, I can see that.

JIM:
The sooner you get it fixed, the sooner we can open, eh?

NATALIE:
Would you like a tea or coffee, Mr Jaffar?

Jim, standing behind the safe engineer, shakes his head violently. Mr Jaffar turns around to catch him in the act. Jim pretends he has a crick in his neck and twists his head around, sucking air in through his teeth.

JIM:
That's better. I've been having terrible trouble with my neck today. I must have slept awkwardly on it last night.

MR JAFFAR:
(to Jim)
That can be nasty.

(to Natalie)
Coffee please - a splash of milk and two sugars.

Mr Jaffar walks over to the safe and looks at the digital timer.

JIM:
So, did you manage to clear up the flood in your kitchen, Mr Jaffar?

MR JAFFAR:
Yes. Would you believe that I've only had the washing machine for a month and it then it floods my kitchen?

JIM:
No, no, I wouldn't. That's totally unbelievable. I wouldn't believe that for

a moment. Not a moment.

Mr Jaffar turns and stares at Jim.

MR JAFFAR:
Well, it's true. I'm lucky it's under warranty, I suppose.

JIM:
Oh yes, lucky. Very lucky. What a lucky man you are. Lu-cky, lu-cky, lu-cky.

Mr Jaffar turns again to Jim. Natalie brings in a coffee for Mr Jaffar. Jim flays his arms out and slaps them down on his sides in exasperation. Mr Jaffar catches him out the corner of his eye. Jim starts rubbing the sides of his thighs.

JIM: (CONT'D)
I've been having terrible difficulty with my... thighs today.

MR JAFFAR:
Slept awkwardly on them, did you?

JIM:
Yes. I must have.

MR JAFFAR:
That's unlucky.

PATRICK:
Unlu-cky, unlu-cky, unlu-cky.

JIM:
Go and clean the toilet, Patrick.

EPISODE 3 - ELECTRIC DREAMS

Jim gives Patrick a look that made him not want to argue.

FADE TO:

ACT 2, SCENE 2. INT. OFFICE [11.10 AM]

SHOT OF JIM'S WATCH. IT SHOWS 11.10 AM.

Mr Jaffar is seated at Jim's desk, drinking his coffee and looking at his phone. He laughs. Jim sits on the other side, staring at him and tapping his fingers in frustration.

MR JAFFAR:

Here, look at that. Brilliant. Where do they get their ideas from?

He shows Jim a video on his phone of a cat playing the piano.

JIM:

Yes, brilliant. (ASIDE) At least it was, 15 years ago.

MR JAFFAR:

Right, I suppose I better get on and have a look at your safe then.

He finishes his coffee and walks over to the safe. He presses a few buttons and turns around.

MR JAFFAR: (CONT'D)

Have you tried to re-set the time on this?

JIM:

(LAUGHS) No, I didn't try that one.

Jim winks at Natalie.

MR JAFFAR:

You should have.

Mr Jaffar looks at his watch and taps the keypad a few times. The time is reset.

JIM:

As simple as that. That's not very secure, is it?

MR JAFFAR:

Not really. This is not what you call a 'top of the range' model. However, you still have to put your six-digit passcode in, so it's not likely anyone could guess what it is…unless it's 1,2,3,4,5,6.

He looks at Jim, who looks embarrassed.

MR JAFFAR: (CONT'D)

It's '1,2,3,4,5,6', isn't it?

Mr Jaffar enters the code and turns the handle to open the safe.

MR JAFFAR: (CONT'D)

There we go. And I didn't even have to open my tool bag. I'll be leaving you now, then. I would suggest, Mr Trueman, that you change your password. Think of something that not any Tom, Dick or Mr Jaffar would guess, eh? I'll email you my invoice.

EPISODE 3 - ELECTRIC DREAMS

JIM:

Thank you. See Mr Jaffar out, will you, Natalie?

Natalie does as requested and Jim sits back down, looking extremely embarrassed. Patrick re-enters the code and the safe opens again.

PATRICK:

That was quick. It wasn't just a case of altering the time on the display,then?

JIM:

Put the cash in the till please and I'll open up.

Jim unlocks the front door and the first customer MRS LAWRENCE (late 40s), enter the shop.

MRS LAWRENCE:

You're new, aren't you?

NATALIE:

Yes. I've only been here for a couple of weeks.

MRS LAWRENCE:

I just want to pick up my gold. My name's Mrs Lawrence.

NATALIE:

Do you have your contract, Mrs Lawrence?

MRS LAWRENCE:

Not with me.

NATALIE:

I'll need it before you take your goods out.

MRS LAWRENCE:
Oh, I only live around the corner. I'll be back in a few minutes.

Mrs Lawrence leaves the shop. Meanwhile, Patrick is attending to another customer, MRS DYNES. He hands over a cross on a chain to her.

PATRICK:
There you go, madam. Thank you very much.

MRS DYNES:
Hold on, this isn't mine.

PATRICK:
It is. One cross on chain.

Patrick shows the customer her contract.

MRS DYNES:
No, I'm sure I bought in a different one.

PATRICK:
Let me weigh it for you.

Patrick weighs the jewellery.

PATRICK: (CONT'D)
See, 17.7 Grams. Just as it says on the contract.

MRS DYNES:
The one I bought in had a little man on it.

EPISODE 3 - ELECTRIC DREAMS

PATRICK:

A little man?

MRS DYNES:

A little man on the cross.

PATRICK:

You mean 'Jesus'?

MRS DYNES:

I suppose so.

PATRICK:

You're not very religious, then?

MRS DYNES:

I am. I go to the Temple at least once a month.

PATRICK:

The 'Temple.'

MRS DYNES:

I'm a Buddhist.

PATRICK:

A Buddhist? I don't wish to be rude, but why does a Buddhist have two crosses - this one and the crucifix that you clearly thought you bought in here.

MRS DYNES:

Ahh, yes, there *is* another one. Maybe that's the one with the little man.

PATRICK:

Yes, the little man. Why do you have them?

MRS DYNES:

I was born Anglican. This one's from my Dad and the other one is from my boyfriend.

PATRICK:

He bought it for you, even though you're a Buddhist?

MRS DYNES:

He doesn't know that. He thinks I'm a Christian. He'd be distraught if he found out. He's quite religious. Anyway, sorry for the confusion. Must be off.

Mrs Dynes leaves the shop. Patrick looks over to Natalie who was listening in.

NATALIE:

That's a new one on me.

PATRICK:

Little man on a cross? Perhaps she calls Buddha, - Big man sitting on a flower?

Natalie laughs and strokes Patrick's arm. Patrick smiles. In walks Mrs Lawrence, again, waving a yellow piece of paper.

MRS LAWRENCE:

Got it!

NATALIE:

That's not ours, Mrs Lawrence. Our contracts are pink.

MRS LAWRENCE:

Oh, silly me. I'll be back in a few minutes with the pink one.

Mrs Lawrence leaves as quickly as she arrived.

PATRICK:

If you don't mind me asking, Natalie, why did you split up with your boyfriend?

NATALIE:

You just did ask.

PATRICK:

Sorry.

NATALIE:

I'm kidding. It was mainly due to his general lack of interest in me. He's a keen sportsman and spent most of his time with his football pals in the winter and cricket pals in the summer. We'd rarely go out unless it was to a sports club do. I realised that I was no more than a piece of arm candy to him.

PATRICK:

I think he's mad. Why wouldn't he want to spend more time with you? I would.

NATALIE:

Ah, Patrick, you're very sweet. I guess I just wasn't enough for him. I mean, how can I, with my glass of raspberry gin, sharp wit and good looks compete with 12 or 13 sweaty, hairy men with limited intellect, an array of facial tattoos and a pub cellar full of lager inside them? One of them owns a pub, you see.

PATRICK:

I'd take you out for a raspberry gin, anytime.

NATALIE:

Oh, Patrick, you are adorable.

PATRICK:

I mean it.

Natalie gives Patrick a peck on the cheek. A shrill voice from the doorway destroys the moment.

MRS LAWRENCE:

I've got it.

Mrs Lawrence presents the pink piece of paper to Natalie.

NATALIE:

It's certainly a pink contract.

MRS LAWRENCE:

Just as you asked.

Mrs Lawrence hands the paper to Natalie.

NATALIE:

But, it's a contract for the repayment of your new dishwasher. And if I may say, you're paying an awful lot of interest.

MRS LAWRENCE:

Oh no, what am I like? I looked in the kitchen drawer, saw a pink piece of paper and grabbed it. I can't keep coming back today, but I'll pop in tomorrow, okay?

NATALIE:

Just remember…

MRS LAWRENCE:

A pawn contract.

EPISODE 3 - ELECTRIC DREAMS

NATALIE:

Yes.

MRS LAWRENCE:

Coloured pink

NATALIE:

Yes.

MRS LAWRENCE:

With 'Trueman's' on the top.

NATALIE:

That's it. Three out of three.

MRS LAWRENCE:

Right. I shall see you tomorrow.

Mrs Lawrence leaves the shop and Natalie looks at the computer monitor.

NATALIE:

Uh oh. She has three contracts in at the moment. I bet you a pound to a penny that she'll bring the wrong one in tomorrow.

PATRICK:

Probably. Anyway, Natalie, about what we were talking about. Would you...

JIM: (O.S.)

Natalie! Can you come in here for a moment, please? I need you to confirm your tax code.

Natalie goes to Jim, leaving Patrick stranded in mid-flow and looking

rather sorry for himself.

FADE TO:

ACT 2, SCENE 3 INT. OFFICE [11.40 AM]

SHOT OF NATALIE'S WATCH. IT SHOWS 11.40.

Natalie is sitting across the desk from Jim.

JIM:
That's sorted.. I'll leave it in the hands of Her Majesty's Revenue Service now. So, Natalie, how are you liking working here?

NATALIE:
It's great. You certainly have an eclectic mix of customers.

JIM:
That's an understatement. I'm glad you're enjoying it. I'm enjoying having you. I mean, having you here.

NATALIE:
I knew what you meant. Actually, do you mind if I stay here a moment longer?

JIM:
Why's that?

NATALIE:
I think that Patrick is about to ask me out

EPISODE 3 - ELECTRIC DREAMS

JIM:

Really?

NATALIE:

I was just telling him about Kit and, well, I may have given him the impression that I am available.

JIM:

Oh dear. You're probably a bit too old for him, really.

NATALIE:

Oh, thanks.

JIM:

What I mean to say is, I think he might be a bit young for you.

NATALIE:

That doesn't make it better, Jim.

JIM:

What I mean to say is - a lady of your elegance and sophistication is out of the league of a pea brained idiot like him.

NATALIE:

Cruel, but better. He plays a good game of chess, though.

JIM:

That part of his brain works fine…more than fine. I don't get it. But, you know what I mean?

NATALIE:

I do.

JIM:

You can go to lunch now, if you like. I need to pop out later to buy myself a new shirt for tonight.

NATALIE:

Oh yes, it's date night, isn't it? What's her name? How did you meet her? Is she your age? How many times have you been out with her? What's she like?

JIM:

Wow. What's this - 20 questions? Her name is Kerry. She's the mother of one of my daughter, Lucy's friends and we met at one of recitals. She's my age and divorced. I've only been out with her once. She's quiet and kind - the polar opposite of my ex-wife. And, do you know what I like the most about her? I love that she's straight-forward, uncomplicated and honest. How about that? I even answered a question you didn't even ask.

NATALIE:

Very good. And where are you taking her?

JIM:

We're trying that new French Bistro on the High Street. I love fine French dining with a decent bottle of Champagne, of course.

NATALIE:

Of course. That sounds perfect, Jim. I'm pleased for you. I wish Kit could have been more like that.

JIM:

You'll find someone else who'll appreciate you.

NATALIE:

I hope so. I think I'd like someone a bit older. Someone I can connect with - like you.

Jim stops in his tracks and is lost for words.

I mean someone your age, with your sensibilities. Not necessarily you.... I mean, not *you* at all.

Not that you're not the sort of guy I'd go for. I mean... I'll be going to lunch now then.

Natalie grabs her handbag and leaves the shop. Jim is left sitting at his desk, mulling over Natalie's confused ramble.

FADE OUT.

END OF ACT TWO

ACT THREE

ACT 3, SCENE 1 INT SHOP. [3 PM]

FADE IN:
SHOT OF TOWN HALL CLOCK. IT STRIKES THREE TIMES.

Jim returns from the menswear shop in a good mood and is whistling. He's carrying a bag and a bottle of white wine. Natalie meets him at the doorway and Jim walks past her, then spins around.

JIM:

Lock up your daughters, Jimbo's back in town.

NATALIE:
Jim—

JIM:
A little aperitif before dinner and look, I'll be irresistible to Kerry in this.

Jim puts the bottle on the floor and pulls out a salmon- coloured shirt out of the bag and holds it up to his neck.

NATALIE:
Jim—

JIM:
As a lady of taste and sophistication, what do you think? Do you like it? Is it a winner? Of course it is.

Jim's ex-wife, VANESSA is standing behind the counter, with arms folded.

VANESSA:
James! Natalie is trying to warn you that your ex-wife is standing behind you and witnessing a quite pitiful display of male machismo.

Jim turns around, quickly, places the shirt back into the plastic bag and picks up the bottle. Vanessa disappears into the office. Jim follows. She stands with her back to the safe; arms folded again.

VANESSA: (CONT'D)
So, who is Kerry - apart from some poor soul you're going to subject your insufferable wit and cheap wine on?

JIM:
She's a lady, I'm taking out to dinner, tonight.

EPISODE 3 - ELECTRIC DREAMS

VANESSA:

Did she accidentally swipe right and end up with you?

JIM:

No! I met her in real life and this isn't the first time that we've been out.

VANESSA:

And she's coming back for more? Incredible. How many times have you seen her?

JIM:

Tonight is our second date.

VANESSA:

She must like you to make it past the first date. But you can't think too much of her - screw top, not a cork? That's rather cheap of you, don't you think?

Vanessa points to the bottle that Jim has placed at the end of his desk.

JIM:

Vanessa, have you come here for a reason or have you had an argument with your toy boy and you want to take out your frustrations on me?

VANESSA:

Not at all. Christopher and I are getting on famously. He's so thoughtful. Only yesterday he called to tell me he'd be late back from work, so to make it up to me, he bought home a beautiful bunch of orchids, a box of Belgian chocolates and a bottle of Merlot, with a cork, of course. No expense spared.

JIM:

That's easy when he's got free reign over your credit card.

VANESSA:

James, we share everything. *Everything.*

JIM:

How wonderful. Now, what do you want?

VANESSA:

No need to be so blunt. I want some money.

JIM:

Oh, what a surprise. Has he maxed out your card? What do you want it for? Don't tell me - you need your eyebrows tattooed? Maybe you've chipped a fingernail and you have to get all your acrylics replaced. No, let me guess, the veneers on your teeth need whitening?

VANESSA:

Your manic cynicism hasn't diminished, has it? In fact, it's for our daughter; she's going away to Cornwall for the weekend with her friends and needs some spending money.

JIM:

Oh yes, she did say.

Jim takes out his wallet and hands over £100 to Vanessa.

VANESSA:

Most generous. Mind you, you saved a bit, on that wine. No, I'm being cruel. This new relationship of yours must suit you.

JIM:

It does. Kerry makes me feel wanted and worthwhile.

VANESSA:

You get this impression from a first date? She *must* be the real deal, then. Right, I must be off.

JIM:

(TO HIMSELF) You've been 'off' for years, love. Vanessa puts the money in her purse and strides to the front door. She turns around.

VANESSA:

I do hope she doesn't cancel with some sort of pathetic excuse at the last minute, James. Let's also hope that she appreciates your brand new pink shirt, you bought especially for the occasion. Oh, and just a word of advice; I wouldn't give her that cheap plonk, I'm sure you'll be able to pick up an almost nearly fresh bunch of flowers from the petrol station. Those, alongside your personality and attention to detail should seal the deal.

Vanessa affects a forced laugh.

JIM:

Thanks for your wisdom, Vanessa. Oh, and the shirt colour is salmon.

VANESSA:

Of course; salmon.

Vanessa leaves the shop.

JIM:

You know something - If ever I'm having a good moment, or I find a sliver of joy or happiness, in she sweeps, stomping her three-hundred pound Jimmy Choos all over it.

Patrick and Natalie look at each other. Jim returns to the office and sits at his desk, before taking out his biscuits.

FADE TO:

ACT 3, SCENE 2. INT. OFFICE. [5.25 PM]

SHOT OF TIME ON DESK PHONE. IT SHOWS 5.25.

Natalie and Patrick are in the shop preparing to close. The phone rings. Jim answers it.

JIM:

Oh, hello Kerry.

Jim sounds cocky and wants everyone to hear his date's voice, so he puts her on speakerphone.

KERRY: (O.S.)

Hi Jim. How are you?

JIM:

Very well, thanks. I'm very much looking forward to tonight. How are you?

KERRY: (O.S.)

I've had an accident.

JIM:

Oh no, What happened - are you injured?

EPISODE 3 - ELECTRIC DREAMS

> KERRY: (O.S.)

No, nothing like that. It's more of an incident than an accident to be fair. My new washing machine has sprung a leak and flooded my kitchen. I'm waiting for a plumber, so I'm afraid I'm going to have to cancel this evening.

Jim looks stunned and doesn't know what to say.

> KERRY: (O.S.) (CONT'D)

Hello? Jim?

Jim picks up the receiver.

> JIM:

I'm here. Well, I suppose it's one of those things. Perhaps another time then?

> KERRY: (O.S.)

Yes, I'll give you a call.

> JIM:

Bye, Kerry.

> KERRY: (O.S.)

Bye, Jim.

Jim hangs up and pauses for a moment.

> JIM:

Right, you two. You can get off home now. I'll close up. It's not like I have anywhere to go now, tonight.

Patrick and Natalie enter the office to collect their coats (and pancake-maker). Jim opens the back door. Natalie gives Jim a consolatory

glance and rubs his arm before she leaves.

Jim puts the pledges and cash in the safe and switches the shop lights off. He shuts the safe and puts his coat on. Just before he can set the alarm, the office lights and computers turn off. It's another power cut.

JIM: (CONT'D)

Oh, perfect. Now, I'm stuck here. Damn this place and it's curse.

Jim looks around skyward. You're in league with *her*, aren't you? Don't try and deny it. I know your game, pal. Oh, I know your game, alright.

Jim takes his coat off and slumps into his chair.

FADE TO:

ACT 3, SCENE 3. INT OFFICE [6.30 PM]

SHOT OF THE SAFE TIME DISPLAY. IT SHOWS 6.30.

Jim is still sitting at his desk, which is lit by a candle; His coat is on and zipped up. He is playing chess with himself.

JIM:

Ah, I've got you now.

He moves his black Knight black to check the white King, leaving the black King exposed and he manages to checkmate himself.

JIM: (CONT'D)

What? How the hell did I manage that? The idiot boy beats me and now I can't even win against myself. It's the curse, again.

Jim notices Mrs Mullaney's Tupperware box on a filing cabinet. Without thinking, he walks over and takes one of the chicken slices. He bites into it.

> JIM: (CONT'D)
> Hell fire! What in is in this?

He grabs the bottle of wine off the desk, frantically twists the top off and swills some wine around his burning mouth before swallowing.

> JIM: (CONT'D)
> And *that* is why I bought a screw top Vanessa. Mind you, she was right. It tastes like crap. Yuk!

With fire in mouth extinguished, he sits back down.

> JIM: (CONT'D)
> What a life. What a bloody life!

He thumps his closed fist down on the desk and miraculously, the lights and computers turn on. He thumps it again, to test that it doesn't reverse the spell. He blows out the candle. Finally, he sets the alarm and exits the shop, leaving his new shirt in the bag beside the desk.

> FADE TO:

ACT 3, SCENE 4. INT JIM'S CAR. [6.40 PM]

THE CAR CLOCK SHOWS 6.40. IT IS DARK AND RAINING.

Driving home, Jim stops at traffic lights and through the rain-lashed windscreen and spies the lights of a fish and chip shop, 100 yards away.

JIM: (V.O.)

Mmmm. Fish and chips. I haven't had that in ages. Just a small cod and chips, I think. No, make that a large cod and large chips, mushy peas…and a pot of curry sauce… and a pickled gherkin. All washed down with a bottle of brown ale.

Yes, that knocks all that poncey French crap and an overpriced bottles of fizz into a cocked hat.

Jim parks up and from the streetlights, he watches happy couples walking along under umbrellas. He glances into the chip shop and into the eyes of the female assistant behind the counter meet his. She smiles at him; he smiles back. She smiles even wider.

JIM: (V.O.)

It might not be such a bad night after all.

Jim exits his car, walks across the road in to the chip shop and is greeted by the happy assistant.

FADE OUT.

END OF EPISODE

Episode 4 - Hot In The City

Written by Elliot Stanton

ACT ONE

ACT 1, SCENE 1. INT. CAR [8.35 AM]

SHOT OF THE CAR CLOCK. IT SHOWS 8.35.

It's an unseasonably hot Autumn morning and Jim is sweltering in his car at a set of red traffic lights. He winds his window down, but instead of fresh air, his nose is assaulted by the choking white smoke.

JIM: (V.O.)
Who on earth starts a bonfire at half- past eight in the morning? (SNIFFS) And if I'm not mistaken, there's an undertone of rubber tyre too. It's disgraceful.

He winds his window up and turns on the aircon. Air comes out of the vent, but it's warm.

JIM:
Oh, that's all I need. It worked fine in the summer.

He winds down the window again, only slightly and takes exaggerated

intermittent breaths. The woman in an adjacent car catches Jim make his goldfish impersonation. The lights turn green and he drives off. The radio station airs an advert for the following year's summer holidays.

JIM: (CONT'D)

Summer, next year? People have just come back from their summer hols, *this* year. Not that I did, of course. Mind you, if global warming continues and we keep getting this weather in October, then they'll be no need to go to sunnier climbs. Why would you want to go away if you have all this?

He splutters as the still smoky air enters the car.
Jim parks up at the rear of the shop and enters the premises. As soon as he disables the alarm and switches the lights on, he hears a knock on the front door. It's NATALIE. He lets her in.

JIM: (CONT'D)

Morning.

NATALIE:

Oh, Jim, you look hot.

Jim looks stunned, assuming that Natalie is in full-flirt mode already.

JIM:

What?

NATALIE:

You're sweating. Sorry.

JIM:

Oh, the aircon is broken. And I'm perspiring. Pigs and Patricks sweat, gentleman perspire and ladies glow.

Natalie looks to the heavens and walks past Jim and into the office.

> JIM: (CONT'D)
>
> It's all down to global warming, you know.

> NATALIE: (O.S.)
>
> What's that?

> JIM:
>
> Heatwaves in October. I'm not happy about it.

> NATALIE: (O.S.)
>
> Not to sound rude, Jim, but when are you *ever* happy? I can't remember the last time I saw you laugh.

> JIM:
>
> Oy! I'm happy…sometimes. I laughed last week - you remember when that blind man's guide dog walked into the phone mast. That was funny.

Jim walks into the office.

> NATALIE:
>
> Oh yes. Poor thing. I remember. I also remember the dirty looks you got from passers-by.

> JIM:
>
> It was funny, alright - a seeing-eye dog who can't see?

Natalie gives him the brush off.

> JIM: (CONT'D)
>
> Okay, I'm a cruel man.

EPISODE 4 - HOT IN THE CITY

NATALIE:

You are. Tea?

JIM:

Actually, I'll have a coffee this morning,

Natalie goes into the kitchen. There is a slap of soapy rag on window from the front of the shop. The window cleaner, GEORGE, beckons Jim towards him. Jim opens the front door.

JIM: (CONT'D)

Hello George.

GEORGE:

Good morning. Here, you know I'm not one to gossip, but I saw something just now, I thought I should tell you about.

JIM:

Oh yeah, what's that, then?

GEORGE:

I saw your boy, Patrick, up the road.

JIM:

Really, George? He's probably on his way here. You know… to work. Your stories are getting spectacularly dull of late.

GEORGE:

I saw him…with someone.

JIM:

With someone?

GEORGE:

Yes.

JIM:

Is that it?

GEORGE:

He was *with* a female, in a romantic embrace. Kissing.

JIM:

Really? (SHOUTS TO NATALIE). Here, Natalie, George here has just seen our Patrick snogging the face off a young bird.

GEORGE:

That's the thing - she wasn't young.

JIM:

Really?

Natalie joins the two men.

GEORGE:

I couldn't tell exactly how old she was from where I was standing, but she certainly not in the first flush of youth.

NATALIE:

Oooh, so Patrick likes an experienced lady, eh?

JIM:

Someone who's been around the block a bit. Someone with a few miles on the clock.

NATALIE:

Misogyny lives and breathes.

GEORGE:
Shhh! Here he comes.

PATRICK approaches the shop entrance. Jim, Natalie and George step aside to let him in.

PATRICK:
I'm getting a guard of honour now, am I?

JIM:
Good morning, Patrick.

NATALIE:
Good morning, Patrick.

GEORGE:
Alright?

PATRICK:
What's going on? Have I missed something?

JIM:
Not that I've heard of, but if you have, I'm sure she would have steered you in the right direction?

PATRICK:
What *are* you on about? I think the sun has got to your head.

Patrick disappears into the office. Natalie and Jim laugh, George gets back to cleaning the windows.

NATALIE:

That's better, Jim. You're laughing - albeit at someone else's expense.

JIM:

Natalie, all humour is at someone or something else's expense. Now where's that coffee?

Jim and Natalie walk towards the office.

FADE TO:

ACT 1, SCENE 2. INT SHOP [10.30 AM]

SHOT OF TIME ON THE COMPUTER. IT SHOWS 10.30.

Patrick is in the shop, while Jim and Natalie are chatting about him in the office.

NATALIE:

Who can it be and why has he kept it quiet from us?

JIM:

It's probably some old brass.

NATALIE:

Jim!!

JIM:

Well, it might be. Anyway, being serious for a moment, I have something else on my mind.

EPISODE 4 - HOT IN THE CITY

NATALIE:

Jim, you dirty boy.

JIM:

You know me so well. No, Vanessa came around yesterday, completely out of the blue. She told me she wants to sell half her share of the business.

NATALIE:

No! Why?

JIM:

'I want to release some funds for other activities,' she put it.

Meaning, a tummy tuck, a few little treats for her toy boy and get this - a home spa room, whatever *that* is.

NATALIE:

And how do you feel about that?

JIM:

I don't know. On the one hand, she'll have much less say in the business, but on the other hand, who knows who she'll sell it to and what will they will want to do. In our partnership contract, it gives no partner the power to veto a sale. What would you do if you were in my position?

NATALIE:

That's a tricky one. I'm not sure if I'm qualified to advise.

JIM:

I'd value your advice, Natalie.

NATALIE:

I'd certainly want to know if I can work with any new partner and what their plans for the business were.

JIM:

That may be easier said than done. However, knowing Vanessa, it'll take her so long to find a buyer, she'll simply just go off the idea.

NATALIE:

But then, you'll be stuck with her again.

JIM:

It's a win/win, lose/lose situation.

NATALIE:

It is, a bit.

A customer enters the shop.

PATRICK: (O.S.)

Jim! Someone is here to see you. It's Mrs Spillett.

JIM:

Oh no, not her.

NATALIE:

Who's she?

JIM:

I thought she'd gone for good. She's an old customer who's been after me for years. She's always trying to get me to take her out or worse. And I really don't want to.

NATALIE:

Why?

JIM:

She scares me. You don't know what an effort it's been to ward her off. I'm the Van Helsing to her Dracula. She'd love to sink her teeth into me.

PATRICK: (O.S.)

Jim!

JIM:

Wish me luck. If you hear me clear my throat loudly, come and rescue me. If you don't, it'll mean that she already has her fangs in it.

Jim gets up to greet Mrs Spillett.

JIM: (CONT'D)

Mrs Spillett, what a nice surprise. It's been ages since we last saw you.

MRS SPILLETT:

Hello, Jim. I know, I've been looking after my mother in Scotland.

JIM:

(UNDER HIS BREATH) Don't you mean Transylvania?

(TO MRS SPILLETT) Oh, how is she? I remember you saying she was over the worst.

MRS SPILLETT:

She was, but then she regressed. She died.

JIM:

(TO PATRICK) Ran out of crosses, garlic and silver bullets, did she?

(TO MRS SPILLETT) Oh, I am sorry to hear that. My deepest condolences.

MRS SPILLETT:

It happens to us all. Now, Jim, I want to ask you something.

JIM:

Mrs Spillett, I'm afraid I won't be able to take you out any time soon as I too, am the sole carer to *my* poor mother now too and caring for her takes up all my spare time.

MRS SPILLETT:

I thought you had her put in a care home? I remember you saying that you'd been trying since she was in her 40s.

JIM:

Yes, that was my little joke. I still have to bring her things and sit with her a lot… a bit

MRS SPILLETT:

My heart bleeds for you. No, I wasn't going to ask you out, Jim. That ship has well and truly sailed for you. You had your chance. What I want to ask you is if you'd be interested in buying some of my late mother's jewellery?

JIM:

Oh. Well, yes, of course. We're always interested in buying jewellery.

MRS SPILLETT:

Good. I haven't got it with me now. I didn't want to bring it out just on the off chance and by the look at some of the shirtless, tattoo-laden characters out there, I'm glad I didn't. I shall be along later in the week.

JIM:

That's absolutely fine. I look forward to that.

MRS SPILLETT:

I'm sure you do. I'll see you then. Bye, Jim. Goodbye, Patrick.

PATRICK:

Goodbye Mrs Spillett.

Mrs Spillett leaves and Natalie comes out into the shop.

NATALIE:

That's a bit lucky, eh, Jim?

JIM:

I guess so, but why doesn't she fancy me anymore? She couldn't get enough of me before. Have I changed that much?

PATRICK:

Maybe she's evolved.

JIM:

Evolved? Thank you, Charlie Darwin.

NATALIE:

Maybe she couldn't wait any longer and had to settle for someone not quite as suave and sophisticated as you.

JIM:

You hear that, Patrick? That's the sort of answer I expect from my staff. Thank you, Natalie.

Jim and Natalie return to the office, leaving Patrick in the shop.

FADE TO:

ACT 1, SCENE 3. INT. OFFICE. [11.15 AM]

SHOT OF JIM'S WATCH. IT SHOWS 11.15.

Jim is on the office phone.

JIM:

(ON PHONE)Yes, Mrs Khan. Please don't worry... No, it's still here... I can see it in the safe right now... No, I won't sell it. You're not overdue. Please don't worry, Mrs Khan... Okay, I'll see you soon. Goodbye, Mrs Khan.

Jim slams down the phone.

JIM:

Boy, if I've told her once, I've told her a thousand times.

PATRICK: (O.S.)

Natalie! Something's arrived for you!

NATALIE:

Again? He doesn't give up.

Jim follows Natalie into the shop. Patrick hands her an envelope, which she hesitantly opens.

NATALIE: (CONT'D)

Wow, it's a two hundred pound gift voucher for Harrods. (READS) *This is just a small token of my undying affection. Do with it as you please. Kit x*

JIM:

Send it straight back. Mind you, he's not afraid of spending his money on you, is he?

PATRICK:

Two-hundred pounds - a *small* token? My Great-aunt gave me a ten-pound WH Smith voucher last Christmas and I haven't heard the end of it. 'Have you spent it yet? *Why* haven't you spent it? If you don't need it, I'll have it back.'

Jim and Natalie ignore him.

JIM:

You know he's trying to buy your affection, don't you?

NATALIE:

Sort of, but at least he's making an effort.

JIM:

And, of course, you'll be able to go on a little spending spree in Harrods?

NATALIE:

If I accept it, of course.

JIM:

If you accept it.

Natalie stares at the gift card and reads Kit's message, again. Jim goes back into the office.

END OF ACT ONE

ACT TWO ACT 2, SCENE 1. INT. OFFICE 1. PM

SHOT OF JIM'S WATCH. IT SHOWS 1. PM.

Jim is sitting at his desk, fretting about Vanessa's announcement. Natalie is opposite him, thinking about what to message Kit. Jim looks up and notices Patrick, talking to a lady in the shop.

>JIM:

Here, do you think that this is her?

Natalie leans forward to take a peak.

>NATALIE:

It could be. She looks older than him, but not *that* much older.

>JIM:

Shall I take a closer look?

>NATALIE:

No…not yet. What are they talking about?

>JIM:

I can't hear. It all a bit hush-hush. Maybe he's inviting her back to his place tonight?

>NATALIE:

To sit around the TV, watching Midsommer Murders with his parents and sister?

>JIM:

Or perhaps a dirty weekend away?

NATALIE:

Yes, that will be it. If it's not Midsommer Murders, it must be a weekend of carnal interaction.

JIM:

Well, it's bound to be. She's gorgeous. Totally out of his league, of course. Very professionally dressed too. I'm going to intervene.

NATALIE:

Be tactful, Jim.

JIM:

Tact is my middle name.

NATALIE:

I thought it was 'Bullinachinashop.'

Jim silently slithers into the shop and stands behind Patrick. The woman stops in her tracks, alerting Patrick to Jim's presence.

JIM:

Everything alright, Patrick?

PATRICK:

Yes, thank you.

JIM:

I saw you talking to this lovely lady and I thought that perhaps you'd like some assistance.

PATRICK:

No, not at all.

JIM:

I see. You're still trying to keep this under your hat, eh? I understand. I suppose you don't want to expose your *friend* to all and sundry yet. It's early days, eh?

Patrick secrets a gift back away from Jim's eyeline. And the lady picks up some money from the counter and puts it in her bag.

PATRICK:

Er, this is Angela.

JIM:

Hello, Angela. Pleased to meet you.

ANGELA:

Hello Jim. I was just…

Patrick coughs loudly on purpose, cutting Angela short.

JIM:

I won't pry. Except to say, that I think Patrick has exceptionally good taste.

PATRICK:

Jim…

JIM:

Just don't lead this one astray. He's lead a very sheltered life.

PATRICK:

Jim…

JIM:

I hope you don't mind fried chicken or slumming it at the local chippy? Patrick's idea of fine-dining isn't up to much. It's a shame, as you look like a lady of taste and refinement.

Angela, looks confused, but puts her professional face on.

ANGELA:

Ah, that's good of you to say. Perhaps I could interest you too.

Jim is taken aback.

JIM:

I beg your pardon?

ANGELA:

It's not exclusive to just Patrick. It's available to everyone.

JIM:

Everyone?

ANGELA:

Absolutely. Men, women, old, young, anyone. There's plenty to go around. Would you like to have a little peak, Jim? I've got plenty to show you.

JIM:

I'm not sure if that's appropriate.

PATRICK:

Go on, Jim, let Angela show you her wares.

Jim stands stunned, while Angela puts her bag down. She reaches into her bag and takes out a couple of plastic tubes and a glass jar full of a white cream.

PATRICK: (CONT'D)
I bought some of Angela's skin cleansing regimen for my Mum. You'll buy some too, won't you, Jim?

Jim looks very embarrassed.

JIM:
Er…yes. Of course.

ANGELA:
I haven't even explained how it works or how much it costs.

JIM:
I'm a bit busy, Angela. I'll get Patrick to fill me in on the details later. How much is it?

ANGELA:
Well, the normal RRP is fifty pounds for a tube of cleanser and the pot of moisturiser, but I'm offering both for twenty-five pounds today and that comes with a free tube of antioxidant serum. What that does is this…

JIM:
Twenty-five pounds, you say?

Jim takes out his wallet and hands over the money. Angela puts the products into a presentation bag and places it in the drawer under the counter. Jim picks up the bag and smiles embarrassed at the saleswoman before going back to the office.

PATRICK:
He's a busy man, Angela.

ANGELA:

So it appears. Anyway, I must be off. Thanks, Patrick.

Angela leaves the shop and Patrick goes into the office.

JIM:

Thanks for that, Patrick. You made me look a right tit.

PATRICK:

Its all your fault, Jim. You assumed that she was my girlfriend and then set about acting like a complete idiot.

JIM:

You could have stopped me.

PATRICK:

I could have, but I didn't want to. 'He's had a sheltered life' indeed.

JIM:

So, who *is* this mystery woman, then? You have to tell us now.

PATRICK:

No, I don't. And if you don't mind, I'll go to lunch.

Patrick leaves and Natalie sits back, shaking her head at Jim.

JIM:

How was I supposed to know?

NATALIE:

And that makes it better?

JIM:

Well, he shouldn't have secrets from us. Who *is* this mystery woman? I'm determined to find out. Having secrets isn't good for you.

VANESSA:

Oh, I don't know. I think one needs an air of mystery.

Jim's ex-wife Vanessa appears as if by magic in the shop.

JIM:

Bloody hell, woman. Where did you come from?

VANESSA:

From the pits of Hades, so you've often told me, James. And it's hot enough outside to feel like I'm still there.

JIM:

Jeez; she's developed a sense of humour too.

VANESSA:

You always complained I didn't have one, now I have one, and you still complain.

Vanessa walks around the counter and into the office. Natalie vacates her chair and Vanessa sits down.

VANESSA: (CONT'D)

(TO NATALIE) Be a love and make me a coffee, will you?

JIM:

Make yourself one.

EPISODE 4 - HOT IN THE CITY

VANESSA:
Ooh, have I touched a nerve?

JIM:
Vanessa! There's a pause.

VANESSA:
I'm sorry, Natalie. I was being rude.

NATALIE:
It's okay; I was going to make one anyway.

Natalie disappears into the kitchen and puts the kettle on.

VANESSA:
(WHISPERS) About me selling half of my share.

JIM:
You don't have to whisper, Natalie knows.

VANESSA:
Of course, she does.

JIM:
Have you changed your mind then?

VANESSA:
Not at all. I came by to tell you that I have some news - some good news. I've found a buyer.

JIM:
What? Already? How did you manage that?

VANESSA:

I was talking to Penelope this morning.

JIM:

Oh, don't tell me, she and Trevor have a friend who has a friend?

VANESSA:

Even better than that.

JIM:

What do you mean?

VANESSA:

She's going to buy half of my share. Penelope and Trevor are going to be our new business partners.

JIM:

You've *got* to be joking? *She* spends money like it's going out of fashion and *he* gives it to her in a vain attempt to repair the pulled sinews of their sham of a marriage.

VANESSA:

And?

JIM:

And? And you think that the business will be in safe in the hands of Lord and Lady Spendalot?

VANESSA:

Trevor is the owner of a very successful and profitable bathroom installation company.

EPISODE 4 - HOT IN THE CITY

JIM:

Which his wife has nothing to do with, otherwise... otherwise...er...

NATALIE: (O.S.)

Otherwise, the profits would be flushed down the khazi.

JIM:

Yes, thank you, Natalie.

VANESSA:

Don't be silly. I'm sure she'd want nothing to do with the day to day running of the shop.

JIM:

You're sure?

VANESSA:

She has made no suggestion that she would. Besides, where else am I going to find a cash buyer so quickly? In any event, I've given her my word.

JIM:

You gave me your word once. Several words. You remember - ones like richer, poorer, sickness, health, death and part?

VANESSA:

Oh, really, James? You said them too, but then you go and...

JIM:

Alright, we don't need to go over the same old ground again.

Vanessa stands up and with a swish of her dress, goes to leave the shop.

VANESSA:

They're signing the papers tomorrow night. Just try and get used to the idea. We'll speak on the phone.

Natalie comes out of the kitchen, holding a mug of coffee.

NATALIE:

I guess she won't be wanting this, then?

FADE TO:

ACT 2, SCENE 2. INT. OFFICE. [2.15 PM]

SHOT OF OFFICE PHONE. THE DISPLAY SHOWS 2.15.

Jim and Natalie sit opposite each other at the desk. Patrick is behind the counter and into the shop walks the octogenarian, Mrs Mullaney.

MRS MULLANEY:

Cooey, Patrick.

JIM:

(FROM OFFICE) Hello Elaine. I won't be a minute.

MRS MULLANEY:

No, it's okay. I've come to see Patrick today.

EPISODE 4 - HOT IN THE CITY

JIM:

Oh, okay then.

Jim and Natalie can hear Patrick whisper and laugh together.

JIM: (CONT'D)

What's going on there?

NATALIE:

I don't know.

JIM:

Oh, God, you don't think.

NATALIE:

No!!

JIM:

An older woman?

NATALIE:

There's old and there's ancient. She's almost four times his age.

JIM:

Shhh! I'm trying to hear what they're talking about.

MRS MULLANEY (O.S.)

Oh, Patrick, that's lovely. You certainly know your stuff.

PATRICK: (O.S.)

I aim to please, Mrs Mullaney.

MRS MULLANEY (O.S.)

Call me Elaine. After all, we know each other pretty well now, don't we?

They both giggle.

JIM:

I think I'm going to be sick.

NATALIE:

Shhh! Now *I* can't hear.

MRS MULLANEY: (O.S.)

I want to thank everything you've done for me, Patrick. I feel like you've taught me so much.

PATRICK: (O.S.)

No, it's you who've taught me things... Elaine.

JIM:

This has got to be stopped. It's insane, immoral and if not illegal, it bloody well should be.

Jim gets up and strides into the shop.

MRS MULLANEY:

Sorry, I can't stop today, Jim. And I'm sorry I haven't got anything for you.

JIM:

No, I think Patrick has had quite enough already. And to be frank, he's welcome to it.

Oblivious to Jim's outburst, Mrs Mullaney prepares to leave. Patrick looks at Jim with a confused expression.

MRS MULLANEY:

Bye, you two. And thanks again, Patrick.

She gives Patrick a little wave as she leaves the shop. Jim folds his arms and stares at Patrick. Patrick stares back.

JIM:

Oh, Patrick. What are you doing? What *are* you doing?

PATRICK:

Just helping out an old lady.

JIM:

Helping out? That's how you justify it?

PATRICK:

Why? I think I did a good thing. She wanted to ask you, but didn't think you were up to it.

JIM:

Well, she wasn't far off the mark. I don't think I'd ever be up to it - or up *for* it?

PATRICK:

For what its worth, I think her grandson will be happy with what she bought him.

JIM:

Pardon?

PATRICK:

The tablet.

JIM:

The tablet?

PATRICK:

Mrs Mullaney wanted to buy a tablet for her grandson for Christmas. He's coming over from New Zealand for the holidays and I've been giving her advice on what one to buy.

JIM:

Well, that's alright, then.

PATRICK:

Hold on, You didn't think…

Jim looks away.

PATRICK: (CONT'D)

Oh, for heaven's sake -you're a sick man, Jim. A sick, sick man.

JIM:

Well, with all the secrecy and whispering, what was I supposed to think?

PATRICK:

She's over 80 years old!

JIM:

I know, but it was you who told us that you're seeing an older woman.

PATRICK:

An older woman, not an *old* woman - not a woman even *you* would think was old.

JIM:

So, who is she, then? Do we know her?

PATRICK:

I'm not getting into this with you. I'm going to the toilet.

JIM:

Of course, you are.

Natalie enters the shop.

NATALIE:

You handled that with great tact and panache, Jim.

Natalie exits the shop, back into the office, leaving Jim alone to dwell on Natalie's words.

FADE TO:

ACT 2, SCENE 3. SHOP. [2.45 PM]

SHOT OF CLOCK ON COMPUTER SCREEN. IT SHOWS 2.45.

A young girl of about ten years old enters the shop and tentatively walks up to Jim at the counter.

JIM:

Hello, young lady. What can I do for you?

YOUNG GIRL:

I need to get my Mum's chain out.

JIM:

I'm afraid your Mum needs to come in and get it herself, with her contract.

YOUNG GIRL:

I've got the paper. Look.

The young girl pulls up a tightly folded pink contract from her trouser pocket.

JIM:

She still needs to come in for herself.

YOUNG GIRL:

She can't. She's in hospital.

JIM:

I'm sorry to hear that, but I'm afraid you have to be an adult to collect a pledge.

YOUNG GIRL:

Can my sister come in and get it?

JIM:

Is she an adult?

YOUNG GIRL:

She's a grown-up.

JIM:

In that case, she can.

EPISODE 4 - HOT IN THE CITY

YOUNG GIRL:

I'll just go and get her.

The girl folds the contract up again and puts it in her trouser pocket. She leaves the shop. Jim waits at the counter. A few seconds later, the girl comes back with an older girl. They approach Jim.

OLDER GIRL:

I've come to get my mum's chain out.

JIM:

And how old are you?

OLDER GIRL:

I'm 16…nearly.

JIM:

You have to be 18 years old to take it out.

OLDER GIRL:

But my mum's in hospital.

JIM:

So, I hear. That's unfortunate, but it's the law, I'm afraid. Is there an adult (LOOKS AT YOUNG GIRL) who is over 18 years of age, your mum can ask?

OLDER GIRL:

I'll have to ask her.

Both girls leave the shop. Jim turns around, about to go into the office, when the front door opens again. The two girls enter, followed by an unkempt woman in a pink tracksuit holding a sausage roll in one hand and the pink contract in the other. She approaches Jim.

WOMAN:
I'd like to get this out.

JIM:
You know these girls?

WOMAN:
Of course. They're my daughters.

JIM:
They said their Mum was in hospital. But by looking at the bag your sausage roll is in, you appear to have been… in Gregg's, the bakers.

WOMAN:
Sorry about that. I was going to come in, but it was the lure of the sausage roll…then there was a long queue, so I asked the kids. You understand.

JIM:
Not really.

WOMAN:
So, can I get my chain out?

JIM:
You can.

WOMAN:
Oh, by the way, is Patrick about?

JIM:
No, why?

EPISODE 4 - HOT IN THE CITY

WOMAN:
No reason.

The woman hands over the crumpled, greasy pink contract to Jim. He gives the woman the once over as she takes another messy bite of her sausage roll. The flakes of pastry go everywhere, not that she cares.

JIM:
(UNDER HIS BREATH) Mullaney would be a step up from Waynetta Slob. Please don't let it be her -for the boy's sake.

Jim looks up the contract number on the computer.

JIM: (CONT'D)
That'll be £56.50 please, Mrs Rose.

The woman hands over the crumpled, greasy banknotes and Jim goes to get her change and her chain. He gives Patrick, who is checking off the overdue pledges, a look of abject disgust.

JIM: (CONT'D)
There we go. Next time, please come in yourself.

The woman nods, picks up her change and chain and leaves the shop with her children in tow, leaving a trail of flakey pastry in her wake.

JIM: (CONT'D)
Patrick!

Patrick joins Jim.

PATRICK:

Now, before you accuse me of having a relationship with that woman, I'd like to remind you of your pitiful record of deductions today.

JIM:

But she asked for you.

PATRICK:

When I served her last time, she said she preferred to be served by me.

JIM:

Oh, did she now?

PATRICK:

I have what they call, 'simpatico.'

JIM:

You mean 'simplicity'?

PATRICK:

No, simpatico. It means I'm easy to get on with, likeable and I share similar interests with others.

JIM:

So she has interests in American hard rock, spending most of a working day sitting on the toilet and cajoling old women? Having said that, her palate appears to be just as sophisticated as yours.

PATRICK:

Old-*er* women. In fact, and old-*er* woman. Some customers see me as a kindred spirit.

JIM:

Kindred spirit? It's gets better. Look, Just tell me who this mystery woman is and I'll get off your back.

PATRICK:

Jim, you're not going to get anything out of me, so you might as well stop trying. Now, I'm off to the bank, okay?

JIM:

Right - the paying in book's on the desk.

Patrick takes a wad of money out of the safe and picks up the paying-in book and leaves the shop. Natalie joins Jim.

JIM:

'Simpatico'? Just where does he get it from?

NATALIE:

He's determined not to tell you.

JIM:

He'll slip up and when he does, I'll be there to see him fall. No one gets one over Jim Trueman.

NATALIE:

Bloody hell. Listen to yourself. Who do you think you are - JR Ewing?

JIM:

Interesting reference. Besides, if you've got it, honey. Now, be a sweetheart and fetch me a bourbon and branch.

NATALIE:

We've got tea, coffee and water, and you can go and get it yourself.

Natalie storms back to the office. Jim looks like he wished he'd kept his mouth shut.

END OF ACT TWO

ACT THREE ACT 3, SCENE 1 INT. SHOP. [4. PM]

SHOT OF WALL CLOCK. IT SHOWS 4 O'CLOCK.

Jim re-enters the shop. His shirt sleeves are rolled up and he is sweating.

JIM:
It's not right, I tell you.

NATALIE:
What?

EPISODE 4 - HOT IN THE CITY

JIM:

Temperatures like this in October. We're just not prepared for it in this country. Wait for the news tonight; I guarantee you they'll be a story about train tracks buckling from the extreme heat. And where are all the ice cream vans when you want one? Typically, at the first sign of a flowering crocus, you can't hear yourself think for the wretched screech of Greensleeves. And why their constant battle with fire engine sirens, just to destroy the tranquillity of suburban London?

PATRICK:

'I've been Jim Trueman; goodnight.'

JIM:

What?

PATRICK:

It sounds like a monologue from your stand-up routine.

NATALIE:

So, it's a bit warm for October. Big deal! And I don't think fire engines sound their sirens just to spoil your peace, Jim.

Natalie storms off into the office. Jim follows.

NATALIE: (CONT'D)

I'm sorry, I didn't mean to snap. I just don't know what to do regarding Kit. I was so determined not to take him back, but he's trying.

JIM:

Yeah, trying to buy your affections. And listening to what you're saying, he's succeeding.

NATALIE:

I'm just thinking I was too harsh.

JIM:
Natalie, don't rush into anything…or Harrods, for that matter. Give it some serious thought. You must be sure he's right for you.

NATALIE:
I will.

VANESSA:
Now he's offering relationship advice?

Vanessa appears at the counter.

JIM:
And there she is again! Do you just manifest to eavesdrop on my private conversations?

VANESSA:
I'm not staying; I'm just on my way to Penelope's. She called me. She wants to talk about; you know what.

JIM:
Vanessa, everyone knows about it.

VANESSA:
Well, I shall let you know of any developments.

As quickly as she arrived, Vanessa was gone.

JIM:
She should carry around a canister of green smoke and perfect her wicked witch laugh.

EPISODE 4 - HOT IN THE CITY

NATALIE:

I'll get you my pretty and your little dog too.

JIM:

Going so soon? I wouldn't hear of it. Why, my little party's just beginning!

NATALIE:

I'm melting! Melting! Oh — what a world, what a world!

Both Natalie and Patrick laugh. Patrick looks on.

PATRICK:

Frankly, my dear, I don't give a damn.

Jim and Natalie stop laughing and look pitifully at Patrick.

PATRICK: (CONT'D)

What? Aren't we doing film quotes?

JIM:

Put the kettle on, Patrick.

Patrick trundles past his colleagues and into the kitchen.

FADE TO:

ACT 3, SCENE 2. INT SHOP. [5.10 PM]

SHOT OF WALL CLOCK. IT SHOWS 5.10.

Patrick is serving a female customer, while Jim and Natalie look on from the office doorway.

                JIM:

What about this one?

                NATALIE:

No, she's too young.

                JIM:

She's still older than Patrick.

                NATALIE:

Only by a couple of years. She's no older than 27 or 28. It's hardly what I'd call an older woman.

                JIM:

She is to him. He's only 22. At that age, I thought that 27 was old.

The shop phone rings and Jim goes into the office to answer it. Vanessa's phone number appears on the caller display. Jim presses the speakerphone button.

                JIM: (CONT'D)

Vanessa.

                VANESSA: (O.S.)

James

EPISODE 4 - HOT IN THE CITY

JIM:

Well, do we have a new partner?

VANESSA: (O.S.)

No.

JIM:

What do you mean 'no'?

VANESSA: (O.S.)

I mean 'no' as in 'no'. She's changed her mind. I bet you're delighted?

Natalie looks on as Jim punches the air in delight and pretends to laugh down the phone whilst holding his side. Natalie laughs.

JIM:

No. Not at all. I was coming to terms with the idea.

Jim mimes his nose lengthening like Pinocchio. Natalie laughs again.

VANESSA: (O.S.)

I can't believe she let me down. Do you know the reason?

JIM:

I'm sure I have no idea.

VANESSA:

She's decided she wants a swimming pool. She thinks that with the weather being so hot in October, global warming is here to stay. Trevor agreed there and then. He's such a doormat. I'm not going to get my home spa room now, am I?

JIM:
That is a shame.

Jim flicks Vs at the phone.

VANESSA:
Anyway, I must go. I'm having my eyebrows threaded and pedicure done at six.

JIM:
Make sure you lie down the right way around, or it could all end in a car wreck.

VANESSA:
Goodbye James.

Jim presses the speakerphone button and sits back in his chair with his hands behind his head.

JIM:
And they all lived happily ever after.

NATALIE:
Well, that's made your day.

JIM:
It has. Everything has resolved itself nicely.

NATALIE:
Not everything. We still don't know who Patrick's mystery woman is.

JIM:
That's true, but he's adamant he's not going to tell us. I think we'll just

have to admit defeat on that one. Come on, let's close up and get out of his sweat hole.

> FADE TO:

ACT 3, SCENE 3, INT. JIM'S CAR [5.40 PM]

SHOT OF CAR CLOCK. IT SHOWS 5.40.

Jim is driving and halts at a set of red traffic lights. Roadworkers are relaying the adjacent lane with tarmac.

> JIM:

Jeez, it's stifling in here.

He lowers his window to let some air in, but the fumes from the hot tarmac make him wretch.

> JIM: (CONT'D)

Oh, for crying out loud. This is torture. I'd rather sweat to death.

He closes the window. Looking across the road, he happens to see Patrick. He's in a clinch with his mystery woman.

> JIM: (V.O.)

Come on, turn around! Turn around!

The lights turn to green, but Jim is still waiting to see who the woman

is. **The car behind him hoots him. This alerts Patrick and the woman, who both look around.**

JIM: (V.O.)
Mrs Spillett! I don't believe it.

Patrick and Mrs Spillett see Jim staring at them. He acknowledges them with a nod, before driving off.

JIM: (V.O.)
Well, fancy that. She couldn't have Jim, so she's dropped down the ladder of evolution and ended up with Patrick. It's not been a bad day, after all.

Jim wipes drips of sweat out of his eyes.

JIM'S CAR DISAPPEARS DOWN THE ROAD AND OUT OF SHOT

END OF EPISODE

Episode 5 - Party Fears Two

Written by Elliot Stanton

ACT ONE

ACT 1, SCENE 1. INT. CAR [8.45 AM]

SHOT OF CAR CLOCK. IT SHOWS 8.45 AM

JIM is in a bad mood and the stop/start traffic is making him late for work, so he picks up his mobile to call Patrick to inform him. He brakes hard at a zebra crossing as a man in a wheelchair with his outstretched leg in plaster, wants to cross the road. The sudden halt causes him to drop his phone. Reaching down to pick it up, he accidentally toots his horn with his arm.

EPISODE 5 - PARTY FEARS TWO

MAN IN WHEELCHAIR:
Alright, alright, pal. I'm going as quickly as I can. It's not easy in this.

JIM:
I didn't mean to hoot you.

MAN IN WHEELCHAIR:
I didn't choose to break my leg and end up in a wheelchair.

JIM:
I dropped my phone. I didn't mean it.

MAN IN WHEELCHAIR:
People like you make me sick. No patience and no respect for the disabled. I'd like to see you try to get around like this.

The man reaches the other side of the road and Jim gets hooted himself.

JIM:
(SHOUTING) It was an accident! An accident! Anyway, you're not 'disabled'; you'll walk again.

MAN IN WHEELCHAIR:
Who do you think you are - Jesus of Nazareth? If I could cast this chair away and walk, I would, you idiot.

The man gives Jim the two-fingered salute.

JIM:
Ignorant bastard. I keep telling you I didn't mean it. Oy, are you deaf, pal?

MAN IN WHEELCHAIR:

I can hear you. You don't know when to stop, do you? Do you hate disabled people that much? You're just a ignorant bigot. You'll get your comeuppance. You'll see.

JIM:

Well, it looks like you've already had yours, you moron!

The car behind Jim gave him another hoot. Jim drives off.

JIM: (V.O.)

What an moron. I said I was sorry. At least, I think I did. It's not like I did it on purpose. I'm no bigot, although for him, I'd gladly make an exception.

FADE TO:

ACT 1, SCENE 2. INT. SHOP. [8.55 AM]

SHOT OF JIM'S WATCH. ITS SHOWS 8.55 AM

Jim opens the front door and lets PATRICK and NATALIE in.

JIM:

You two are early.

PATRICK:

Only by five minutes.

JIM:

Then you're five minutes early.

EPISODE 5 - PARTY FEARS TWO

NATALIE:

We can go away and come back in five minutes, if you like.

JIM:

Four minutes.

NATALIE:

Pardon?

JIM:

Four minutes. It was five minutes before you started yapping.

PATRICK:

You're being very pedantic.

JIM:

No, I'm not. I'm just stating a fact. I'm not arguing with you. I've already had my fill and it's not even nine o'clock.

NATALIE:

You better let us get on, Jim, or we'll just be three minutes early. (TO PATRICK) Nice way to start a day.

Patrick and Natalie file past Jim and walk into the office. Jim locks the front door. George, the window cleaner, appears.

GEORGE:

Hold up. I'll do the insides for you today if you like. They look like they need a good going over.

Jim lets him in and is immediately caught up in a conversation he didn't want.

GEORGE: (CONT'D)

Look at that. The mucky gits. Fingerprints and smears all over the place - sweets, chip fat, spittal, hand cream, snot. I can tell precisely what each residue is by it's form and density.

JIM:

(SARCASTICALLY) That's fascinating and surprisingly appetising.

GEORGE:

You may mock, but it's a gift of the window cleaner. When you've worked on windows for as long as I have, you learn a thing or two. I can even tell the difference between animal fat and vegetable oil when it's wiped over glass. Can you?

JIM:

Can you?

GEORGE:

Oh yes. But do you know what the worst thing I find on windows is?

JIM:

I'm sure I don't know.

GEORGE:

Try and guess?

JIM:

I really don't know.

GEORGE:

Just guess, for crying out loud.

EPISODE 5 - PARTY FEARS TWO

JIM:

Erm, blood? Bronchial mulch? Human excrement?

GEORGE:

Good heavens, man! What's wrong with you? No, it's slime.

JIM:

Slime?

GEORGE:

Yes, that horrible fluorescent mess that kids buy now. Who in their right mind would allow their child to walk around, putting their fingers into that muck? It's disgusting.

Disgusting, I tell you.

JIM:

I suppose it is.

GEORGE:

What's the matter with you today? You have that permanently pissed-off look about you.

JIM:

That's because I *am* permanently pissed- off, George. It's just another day in the life of Jim Trueman. It starts badly and goes downhill fast.

GEORGE:

That's down to your attitude and frame of mind, you know. I'm in my 80s and I still I wake up six days a week at 5.30; I do my stretches, eat a bowl of All Bran, do my ablutions and go out on my window round, with a smile and a cheery word for my clients - rain or shine. You need to be a little bit more like me and a little less like these mothers who allow their brats to wipe their filthy little hands over shop windows.

George sets about cleaning the windows, tutting and muttering to himself.

JIM:
I'm sure there's some wisdom in there somewhere, but I'll be damned if I can find it.

Jim walks to the office, where the safe has been opened and three hot mugs of tea are already on the desk.

NATALIE:
What was George on about?

JIM:
Slime, filth and sticky fingers.

PATRICK:
Sounds like my night out, last night.

NATALIE:
Really? You dirty boy. What did you get up to and with who?

PATRICK:
Oh, I didn't get up to anything with anyone. It just thought it was a funny thing to say. I just stayed at home with my parents and watched old episodes of Midsommer Murders on ITV3. They love John Nettles.

JIM:
Patrick, has anyone ever said that you're an idiot?

PATRICK:
Yes, you.

EPISODE 5 - PARTY FEARS TWO

Jim gives him a confused look.

> JIM:
> Yeees. And am I ever wrong?

> PATRICK:
> Frequently.

> JIM:
> What do you mean, 'frequently'?

> NATALIE:
> Boys, let's not go there today, eh?

Jim and Patrick are suitably chastised and drink their tea.

> NATALIE: (CONT'D)
> I thought you'd be happy, now that Vanessa has gone on holiday for a week? No more phone calls or flying visits.

> JIM:
> I should be deliriously happy, shouldn't I? And I was, until last night.

> NATALIE:
> Why, what happened last night?

> JIM:
> I got home to find this.

Jim takes out a card from his jacket pocket.

> JIM: (CONT'D)
> This arrived on my doormat - an invitation - an invitation to Vanessa's 50th birthday, being held at *our* old house and no doubt, to be attended by

our old friends. To make matters worse, it's for me and a 'plus one.' You know what that means, don't you?

PATRICK:

Bloody hell Jim, it means you and a guest. I thought everybody knew that.

JIM:

I know what 'plus one' means, you fool. I was referring to inviting me and a guest.

PATRICK:

I don't follow.

NATALIE:

To be honest, neither do I.

JIM:

It means, either I have to find someone to go with - the poor woman will no doubt be scrutinised at every turn. Or I go alone and I'm subjected to constant jibes from Vanessa that no one wants to be seen out with me. It's a classic double bind.

PATRICK:

A 'what'?

JIM:

Ask your psychiatrist.

PATRICK:

But, I don't have a psychiatrist.

JIM:

Get one!

EPISODE 5 - PARTY FEARS TWO

NATALIE:

Why don't you just decide not to go at all?

JIM:

That is the third and most preferable option. I thought about pretending I didn't receive the invitation and hope she wouldn't remind me until it was too late. Then, I could say I had other plans.

NATALIE:

Why don't you do that then?

JIM:

Two reasons - Firstly, I noticed that there was no stamp on the envelope, so she must have hand-delivered it herself on the way to the airport yesterday and secondly, it's taking place next Saturday night, so no time to plan anything else.

PATRICK:

That's tomorrow week.

JIM:

I realise that, Patrick. She knew exactly what she's doing. She wouldn't pass up a chance like her 50th birthday party to humiliate me. I'll have to think of something.

Anyway, let's get the shop open and see what loonies are on offer today.

FADE TO:

ACT 1, SCENE 3. INT SHOP [9.05 AM]

SHOT OF COMPUTER CLOCK. IT SHOWS 9.05 AM.

It is raining hard and Jim is serving a drenched and bedraggled old man. Rainwater is dripping from his nose. He hands over a soggy contract to Jim.

JIM:
I can just about make out the contract number on this.

Jim looks up the contract number on the computer.

JIM: (CONT'D)
That's going to be £384.87, please.

MR THUROGOOD:
I'm afraid my money got a little wet too.

Mr Thurogood takes out a handful of drenched £20 notes and drops the soggy clump into the drawer. Jim looks horrified.

JIM:
But it's not in your pocket. What happened to it?

MR THUROGOOD:
I was standing outside, waiting for you to open and the rain ran down my coat and into my pocket. That's where I put my contract and money. There's £400 there.

JIM:
You put your money in your coat pocket?

EPISODE 5 - PARTY FEARS TWO

MR THUROGOOD:

'Fraid so.

The customer just nods to the mess in the drawer. Jim picks up two biros and uses them like chopsticks, trying to grab the money with them.

MR THUROGOOD: (CONT'D)

You know, you should get a scraper or something to collect them all at once.

JIM:

(UNDER HIS BREATH) And you, sir, should invest in a wallet...and a brain.

Having retrieved all the notes to the best of the ability, Jim lays them out flat on the back counter.

JIM: (CONT'D)

I'll leave them there to dry for a while. I'll just get your goods and your change.

MR THUROGOOD:

Right ho.

Jim goes to the safe. Natalie is at the desk, folding the overdue letters.

JIM:

If I wasn't sure it was going to be one of those days before we opened, I certainly do now.

NATALIE:

I know, I heard.

JIM:

I mean, who stuffs their money into a coat pocket and stands in the rain waiting for that pocket to fill up with water? What is wrong with these people?

NATALIE:

I would say it's quite a unique decision taken by quite a unique individual.

JIM:

It must be. Natalie, do me a favour, will you? When you're finished, collect the wet notes and leave them on the chair in front of the heater. Not too close, though.

NATALIE:

Yes, Jim. I am aware of the combustible properties of paper when coming into contact with extreme heat.

JIM:

Sorry. Sometimes, I forget I'm not talking to Patrick.

NATALIE:

And how do I remind you of Patrick? Is it my long, dark hair, my smoky, green eyes, my ever-so-slight Spanish accent or is it my long, shapely legs?

Jim stops in his tracks, stunned by Natalie's very flirtatious response.

JIM:

No, no, that's not what I meant. I…I better get this back to Mr Thurogood.

Jim grabs the change and returns to his customer with his goods. He looks behind and Natalie has returned to folding her letters.

JIM: (CONT'D)
Right sir. Err, here's your chain and your change. Fifteen pounds and 13 pence.

Jim's shaky hands almost drop the money before handing it over to Mr Thorogood. To his shock, Mr Thurogood takes out a wallet from his inside his coat and slips the ten pound and five pound notes neatly inside.

MR THUROGOOD:
I don't want the loose change. It'll only weigh me down. Do you have a charity box?

JIM:
Yes sir. We raise money for the desperately hard of thinking.

MR THUROGOOD:
Jolly good. See you, then.

The customer leaves the shop. Jim shakes his head. He once again looks around. Natalie is still folding her letters. He continues to watch her.

FADE OUT.

END OF ACT ONE

ACT TWO

ACT 2, SCENE 1. INT. OFFICE. 12 PM

SHOT OF THE WALL CLOCK. IT SHOWS 12.00.

Jim is sitting at his desk, fanning his face with Vanessa's party invitation. He is watching Natalie, who is sitting on the other side of the desk, stuffing envelopes with the overdue letters.

A customer comes in and Jim goes to greet her. The customer hands over a paper bag of jewellery and Jim starts to sift through it.

JIM:

So, you just want to sell it all?

MRS PINCH:

Yes, they're all bits and pieces that I have no use for anymore. Some items have been in my bedside drawer for years. There are two or three coins in there too.

JIM:

I'm not sure if all or it, or any of it is gold though, but I'll look it over.

MRS PINCH:

I hope it is. Mind you, although I can't remember where most of it came from.

JIM:

Well then, what do we have here? A gold-coloured curtain ring… a ring pull from a can of Coke?

EPISODE 5 - PARTY FEARS TWO

MRS PINCH:

Oh no, we don't drink fizzy drinks.

JIM:

Beer?

MRS PINCH:

Yes, very possibly.

JIM:

Two inches of sink chain…five tiny earrings, none matching, four of which are silver, in colour, and one, coral. What's this - a gold watch bracelet?

Ah, the reverse side has all its colour rubbed away. So, not gold. We're not doing too well, I'm afraid, Madam.

MRS PINCH:

That's a shame.

JIM:

I know. One minute, I think we have some genuine treasure - a ruby and diamond set brooch.

Jim picks up the brooch to take a closer look through his eyepiece.

JIM: (CONT'D)

A-ha!

MRS PINCH:

Is that a good a-ha or a disappointed a-ha?

JIM:

A disappointed a-ha, I'm afraid. What I thought might be an early-eighteenth century, Baroque-style 18ct gold, ruby and diamond set brooch, is, in fact, a late 20th century, Claire's accessories, gold-plated plastic-stone set piece of…

MRS PINCH:
Crap?

JIM:
Well, you said it.

Jim continues to pick through what is becoming a most disappointing treasure hunt.

JIM: (CONT'D)
And this has come out of a Christmas cracker, albeit Waitrose and not Happy Shopper. Well done for that.

Jim tosses aside a silver-coloured plastic ring.

MRS PINCH:
What about the coins, though?

Jim picks up the three coins.

JIM:
There's no doubt that they are indeed coins - well, two of them are. I can confirm that, without hesitation.

MRS PINCH:
That's good…isn't it?

JIM:
Not really. What you have here is an old British halfpenny, a ten peseta coin and a token for a carwash.

EPISODE 5 - PARTY FEARS TWO

MRS PINCH:

I'm sorry about that. I really should have had a closer look before I came out and wasted your time.

JIM:

No, not at all, Madam. It's what we're here for. Hold on a moment...

MRS PINCH:

What? Have you found anything? A little piece of gold? A precious stone?

Mrs Pinch looks excited and Jim takes out his phone from his trouser pocket.

JIM:

Sorry about that. My phone was vibrating in my pocket.

MRS PINCH:

Oh.

JIM:

No, I'm afraid there's nothing here of any value.

Jim grabs the collection and puts it all back into the bag before returning it to Mrs Pinch. She nods and leaves the shop. As she does, a courier comes in with a packet.

COURIER:

Miss Natalie Reyes?

Natalie appears.

NATALIE:

Yes

COURIER:

Package for you, love.

NATALIE:

Oh no, not another one.

Natalie signs for the small padded envelope and stares at it, laying on the counter. The courier leaves.

JIM:

From him, again?

NATALIE:

Yes, I recognise the handwriting.

JIM:

At least it's not another kitchen appliance.

PATRICK:

Unless it's for a doll's house.

Patrick who had appeared at the doorway, looks proud of his 'joke.' The other two ignore him.

NATALIE:

I suppose I'd better open it.

Natalie tears off a strip from the top of the packet and takes out a jewellery box and a piece of paper. She reads the note in silence, before opening the box. Inside is a pair of antique pearl earrings set in white gold.

JIM:

They're beautiful.

NATALIE:

They are. He says they're a family heirloom and he wants me to have them. I can't, of course.

PATRICK:

Why not? I would.

NATALIE:

They wouldn't suit you, Patrick. No, I can't accept them and he knows it.

JIM:

What do you mean?

NATALIE:

He knows I won't accept his gift, as it will suggest I made a mistake. He also knows that I won't want the responsibility of sending them back by post. I'll have to call him. No doubt, he'll give me an encore of the 'Sorry' and 'I can change' routine. There's your double bind again, Jim.

JIM:

So, what are you going to do?

NATALIE:

I'll get my Mum to drop me round there. I'll drop the box through his letterbox. By the time he comes to the door, I'll be back in the car.

JIM:

I can take you, if you like?

NATALIE:

Ahh, thanks. That might be a good idea. I can do without getting it in the ear from my Mum. I'll tell Kit in my lunch-break.

JIM:

What are friends for?

Patrick gives Jim a firm stare.

JIM: (CONT'D)

(TO PATRICK) What?

Jim and Natalie move into the office. Jim begins to stick postage stamps on the letters, while Natalie turns over the drying £20 notes in front of the heater.
The shop phone rings. Jim answers it. It's his daughter, Lucy. He puts her on speakerphone.

JIM: (CONT'D)

Hello, darling. Sorry I didn't answer when you called before; I was with a customer.

LUCY: (O.S.)

Hi Dad. That's alright. I take it you've received the invitation to Mum's 50th?

JIM:

Yes, she hand-delivered it before she went away.

LUCY: (O.S.)

Are you going?

JIM:

I'm trying to find a way to get out of it, to be honest with you.

LUCY: (O.S.)

Oh, don't do that, Dad.

JIM:

Why not?

LUCY: (O.S.)

Because I'll be there and I don't like any of Mum's friends. They're so stuck up.

JIM:

You've noticed? (PAUSES) Oh, okay then. For you. Only For you.

LUCY: (O.S.)

Thanks, Dad. You're the best. Are you bringing anyone?

Jim looks at Natalie, who is still turning the money around.

JIM:

Maybe. I don't know yet.

LUCY: (O.S.)

Okay. See you next Saturday. Bye, Dad.

JIM:

Bye, sweetheart.

Jim presses the button to end the call; his eyes still on Natalie.

FADE TO:

ACT 2, SCENE 2. INT. SHOP. [1.20 PM]

SHOT OF WALL CLOCK. IT SHOWS. 1.20 PM.

A glamourous woman comes into the shop and greets Jim.

MRS GREENWOOD:
Hello, Mr Trueman.

JIM:
Hello, Mrs Greenwood. How are you? Long time, no see.

MRS GREENWOOD:
I know. I've been busy. Come outside, I've got someone I want you to meet.

Jim makes his way around the counter and follows Mrs Greenwood outside the shop. He walks into a throng of several women; including a young woman who has her hands on an old-fashioned pram.

MRS GREENWOOD: (CONT'D)
Everyone, this is Mr Trueman. He's been my saviour on many occasions.

The crowd, to a woman, greet Jim in a very enthusiastic manner.

JIM:
Hello, ladies.

MRS GREENWOOD:
And this is my daughter, Lucy.

The young woman takes her hands off the pram and grabs Jim's hands like he was an old family friend.

EPISODE 5 - PARTY FEARS TWO

JIM:
Hello. My daughter is called Lucy, too.

The woman all coo in delighted amazement.

MRS GREENWOOD:
Oh wow. That's incredible.

JIM:
It's not *that* an unusual name, but I like it, as you do too, Mrs Greenwood.

MRS GREENWOOD:
It's a lovely name. I want you to meet my firstborn grand-daughter. Her name is Hope. She's three weeks old today.

Jim peers into the pram and the baby burps, which makes her look like she's smiling. All the women go wild. Jim is taken aback.

LUCY GREENWOOD:
You have a way with babies, Mr Trueman.

JIM:
I don't know about that. She just burped.

LUCY GREENWOOD:
I think it was a smile. She hasn't smiled before.

Natalie, alerted by the hubbub comes to stand in the doorway to watch the scene. Jim looks uncomfortable.

MRS GREENWOOD:
Go on, Lucy. Let Mr Trueman have a hold.

JIM:

It's okay. I don't want to upset the little thing.

LUCY GREENWOOD:

It's fine. I'll hand her to you.

Lucy Greenwood picks up her child and hands her to Jim. Once again, the child burps and 'smiles', The assembled women let release a chorus of 'oohs and ahhs.'

MRS GREENWOOD:

It's amazing.

LUCY GREENWOOD:

Truly amazing.

NATALIE:

(IN JIM'S EAR) I think they think you're the Messiah.

JIM:

(TO NATALIE) That's the second time today, I've been 'accused' of that.

NATALIE:

(IN JIM'S EAR) Really? But you're not The Messiah. You're a very naughty pawnbroker.

Jim carefully hands back the baby to the young mother and turns to Natalie.

JIM:

That's insubordination, young lady.

EPISODE 5 - PARTY FEARS TWO

NATALIE:
What are you going to do - punish me?

Jim is shocked by Natalie's upping of the ante. Not knowing what to say, he turns back to address Mrs Greenwood and her posse. Natalie returns into the shop.

JIM:
I'm so pleased for you and Lucy and I wish you only happy times ahead.

MRS GREENWOOD:
(TO LUCY). See, I told you he was a gentleman.

LUCY GREENWOOD:
You did indeed. Mum.

MRS GREENWOOD:
A real gentleman. Better than the scumbag who got you pregnant.

LUCY GREENWOOD:
Oh, Mum, please don't keep going on about him. He's long gone now.

Jim stands, looking extremely uncomfortable.

JIM:
Right, ladies, I best get back to work.

He is ignored.

MRS GREENWOOD:
I wish he would have been long gone ten months ago and maybe you wouldn't have ended up the single mother of a newborn baby.

LUCY GREENWOOD:
We're not going over this again, are we? Everyone make mistakes.

JIM:
Err, ladies, I really must go inside.

Once again, Jim is ignored.

MRS GREENWOOD:
It's a pretty big mistake, my girl.

LUCY GREENWOOD:
So, now you're saying that Hope is just a mistake?

MRS GREENWOOD:
That's not what I mean, and you know it.

JIM:
Right, I'm off. Have a nice day now.

Jim leaves the mother and daughter, while the other women continue to stand around watching the display. They don't notice he's gone and continue the bickering.

Jim is back in the office. He and Natalie are watching the continuing argument from a safe distance.

JIM: (CONT'D)
Well, that escalated very quickly.

NATALIE:
They like you though. Almost a God- like reverence.

EPISODE 5 - PARTY FEARS TWO

JIM:

I didn't want to get involved. I didn't want to turn The Messiah into the Anti-Christ.

NATALIE:

You could never be that, Jim. You have a kind heart. You need to learn to let things go sometimes.

JIM:

You think I'm a nice person?

NATALIE:

Definitely. You just need to see it yourself. I'll go to lunch now if that's alright.

JIM:

Yes, of course.

Natalie picks up her handbag and exits the shop. Jim watches her leave.

FADE TO:

ACT 2, SCENE 3. INT. OFFICE [3.10 PM]

SHOT ON JIM'S WATCH. IT SHOWS 3.10 PM

Jim sits at his desk. Patrick sits opposite him. They are drinking coffee. Patrick asks him a question.

PATRICK:
So, what are you going to buy Vanessa for her birthday?

JIM:
Blimey. I hadn't even thought of that yet.

PATRICK:
It'll have to be something expensive for a 50th birthday.

JIM:
Something expensive? She's already got my house and has taken my very soul. Surely, that's worth a few quid.

PATRICK:
You've got to get over that, Jim. It was three years ago.

JIM:
Some scars take longer to heal. I just pray to God that you never have to go through what I did.

PATRICK:
Ahh, thanks, Jim. I'm touched.

JIM:
By the way, I'm agnostic.

EPISODE 5 - PARTY FEARS TWO

PATRICK:

Is that the same as 'atheist'?

JIM:

Not quite. One believes in the existence of God, but not in one religion; the other doesn't believe that there's a God at all.

PATRICK:

That's interesting. I'm a bit undecided, myself. So, which one is which, then?

JIM:

I don't know. To be honest, Patrick, I was just delivering what I thought was a witty and pithy response. I didn't expect you to open up a whole theological debate on the existence of God. Sorry about that.

PATRICK:

'I never apologise... I'm sorry, but that's the way I am.'

JIM:

That's a good one. Rousseau? Descartes? Russell? No, it's got all the hallmarks of Kierkegaard?

PATRICK:

Who? No, it's Homer Simpson.

JIM:

Of course, it was. I was being sarcastic... and a bit facetious. Two for the price of one, there. Right, I think there's a customer who needs serving.

Patrick goes to attend to a customer who has appeared at the counter. Natalie returns from lunch.

NATALIE:

Oh, it's blowing a storm out there.

JIM:

I think we're going to get a bad winter. We won't see the sun for months.

NATALIE:

'No winter lasts forever; no spring skips its turn.'

JIM:

Spongebob Squarepants?

NATALIE:

What? No, Hal Borland. He was an American author and journalist. I love his work.

JIM:

Good. I'm glad to hear that.

NATALIE:

What do you mean?

JIM:

It's just nice to have someone with a little bit of…

NATALIE:

Nous? Intelligence? Wit?

JIM:

All of the above.

NATALIE:

Smoothie. By the way, I called Kit and told him I'd drop off his earrings later on.

JIM:

How did he react?

NATALIE:

He sounded a little taken aback. I reiterated that I didn't want anything from him and I didn't want to get back with him, but I don't think it registers with him.

JIM:

Maybe just try a couple of simple words. If it were a crossword clue it would be something like -*To tell someone, in no uncertain terms, that they should go forth and multiply. Profanity. (4,3).*

Natalie laughs and rubs Jim's arm.

NATALIE:

Nous, intelligence and wit. Care for a coffee

JIM:

Please

Natalie disappears into the kitchen. Jim smiles.

END OF ACT 2

ACT THREE

ACT 3, SCENE 1 INT. SHOP. [4 PM]

SHOT OF A GOLD WATCH THAT JIM IS LOOKING AT. IT SHOWS 4.00.

Jim is looking at a watch that a female customer has bought in.

MISS MCPHERSON:
It just doesn't suit me. I don't wear much gold. I prefer costume jewellery.

JIM:
Each to their own.

MISS MCPHERSON:
I'm forever losing earrings and breaking necklaces, so it doesn't cost me much to replace them. The watch is far too dainty for me. I'd break it in a minute.

JIM:
So, what made you buy it then? Or was it a present?

MISS MCPHERSON:
Neither, I won it in a competition. It was the first prize. In truth, I would have preferred the second prize, which was a garden shed or even the third prize, which was two-year's free pet insurance.

JIM:
What an eclectic selection of prizes. Who put on the contest?

MISS MCPHERSON:

It was the local newspaper. I don't usually enter competitions, but my Dad wanted a new shed.

JIM:

And you wanted…pet insurance?

MISS MCPHERSON:

Yes.

JIM:

Sounds ideal.

MISS MCPHERSON:

Except for the fact that I won the watch.

JIM:

Evidently. Now, how much are you looking for?

MISS MCPHERSON:

I don't expect much. I know its not a well-known brand.

JIM:

No, to be honest, I've never even heard of *Floresay*. It sounds more like a skin condition.

MISS MCPHERSON:

Or a bowel disorder.

They both find their suggestions very funny.

JIM:

Or maybe a shampoo to get rid of nits.

MISS MCPHERSON:
Or a treatment for worms.

JIM:
You could have got Floresay for free had you won the pet insurance.

MISS MCPHERSON:
That's funny.

JIM:
All part of the service, madam. Now, for the value. As you said yourself, it's quite dainty and there's not a great deal of gold weight in it, so, with that in mind and the 'uniqueness' of the brand, I can offer you...sixty pounds.

MISS MCPHERSON:
Really? That's great. I wasn't expecting more than thirty-odd quid.

JIM:
Well, I can re-consider, if you like?

MISS MCPHERSON:
No, no. I'm quite happy with sixty pounds, thank you.

Jim takes the money out of the till and hands it over to the customer.

JIM:
There's your money. Is it going to go towards a new shed, then?

MISS MCPHERSON:
Is it ever? I'm going into town for a night out with my girls, next weekend. It's going to be a riot.

EPISODE 5 - PARTY FEARS TWO

JIM:

Nice. I'm going out next weekend too. It's my ex-wife's 50th birthday party and I'm dreading it. I couldn't tag along with you instead, could I?

MISS MCPHERSON:

I'm sorry. It's strictly ladies only. You wouldn't want to be around me after three or four hours on vodka and cranberry juice.

JIM:

Believe me, it'll still be preferable to what I'll be doing. Anyway, you have a good time.

MISS MCPHERSON:

I will. Tata.

Miss McPherson exits the shop leaving Jim mulling over the coming weekend. He looks down at the watch he just bought.

JIM:

I can see the ad campaign now -
Nothing says, 'Our relationship is hanging by a thread', than giving your undiscerning lady the gift of a Flouresay watch. Flouresay - For When You've Just About Given Up.
Oh damn. I've still got to sort out her present.

Patrick appears on the scene.

PATRICK:

Who for - that woman that just left? Did you disgrace yourself?

JIM:

What are you on about, boy? No. I've got to buy something for Vanessa. Not only does she cost me myself-respect, but she's going to cost me…well, any amount of money spent on a present is money badly spent.

PATRICK:
You could give her that watch.

JIM:
No, I couldn't. When you buy someone a piece of jewellery, it makes a statement. A statement like, 'I love you' or 'I value you.' The statement this watch would make is, 'I couldn't think of anything else to buy' or 'I bought this cheap, from a punter', which is true, of course. Besides, she'd take one look at the brand name, put it back in the box and throw it back in my face

PATRICK:
So, what are you going to get her then? A pancake maker?

JIM:
No, I'm not going to get her a bloody pancake maker, Patrick. It needs to be something not too personal, not too dear, not too cheap, but something that shows at least a modicum of thought.

PATRICK:
Underwear?

JIM:
Patrick, you truly are a buffoon.

Natalie makes her presence known.

NATALIE:
Perfume. It ticks all your boxes. I'm sure she likes perfume. You can't go wrong and it can be impersonal without being unthoughtful.

EPISODE 5 - PARTY FEARS TWO

JIM:

Of course. I'll nip up the road to Superdrug and get something. How much should I pay?

NATALIE:

As long as the RRP is about £50, anything scent that you've heard of. You should give the big pharmacy on the hill a try. They've got a sale on and do some good deals on gift sets. You'll probably find something for about thirty pounds that retails for at least double that. I'd go as soon as I can if I were you as they often sell out.

JIM:

What would I do without you? I'll go now.

Just as Jim is preparing to go, several customers come in and Jim cannot get out.

JIM: (CONT'D)

(To Natalie) We'll just see to this lot and I'll pop up the road.

FADE TO:

ACT 3, SCENE 2. INT SHOP. [4.45 PM]

SHOT OF JIM'S WATCH. IT SHOWS 4.45.

It is raining heavily. Jim is frantically trying to complete a transaction with a customer. Natalie and Patrick are also with customers.

JIM:

There's your contract and your money. Twenty, forty, sixty, eighty, one hundred, one hundred and twenty pounds. Thank you very much. See you soon.

The customer picks up the contract and money and makes her way out of the shop.

JIM: (CONT'D)

Right, if I leave now, I should just make it before they shut.

NATALIE:

Take my umbrella, it's still raining out there.

JIM:

It's alright, it's just a bit of water. I'll survive.

Jim runs into the office and grabs his coat. He returns immediately and runs to the door. He slips on the wet floor and falls into a heap on the ground. He cries out in pain

JIM: (CONT'D)

Arggghhhhh!!!

Natalie runs to his aid. Patrick slowly walks over. The remaining customers stand and stare.

PATRICK:

Are you alright, Jim?

JIM:

No, I'm bloody not alright.

Jim grabs his right ankle.

> NATALIE:
> Can you get up?

Jim tries to get to his feet, but can't. He lets out another shriek.

> NATALIE: (CONT'D)
> We can't leave you down there. Patrick, help me try and lift him onto the chair.

A helpful male customer assists Patrick lift Jim up.

> NATALIE: (CONT'D)
> I'm going to call for an ambulance.

> JIM:
> No, it's alright. I'm sure its just a sprain. I'll be okay in a few minutes.

Foolishly, he tries to stand, but along with another painful shout, he concedes defeat.

> JIM: (CONT'D)
> I was wrong. It's broken!

> NATALIE:
> I think you might be right. I'm calling an ambulance, Jim. End of debate.

Natalie calls 999 and sits with Jim in the shop.

FADE TO:

ACT 3, SCENE 3, INT SHOP. 5 PM

SHOT OF PARAMEDIC'S PHONE. IT SHOWS 5 PM.

One of the paramedics, Michelle, is attending to a prostrate Jim. He winces in pain as she prods his ankle.

JIM:

It's broken! It's broken!

MICHELLE:

It hasn't swelled up yet, so I don't think it is. You may have just twisted it. I do think it needs to be x-rayed, though. It's a trip to the hospital for you.

JIM:

As if things couldn't get any worse. I'm afraid I won't be able to take you to return the earrings tonight, Natalie.

NATALIE:

Oh, don't be silly. You're much more important.

Jim looks up at Natalie.

JIM:

Am I really?

NATALIE:

Of course you are.

JIM:

That's good to KNOOOOOOWWWW!

Jim screams in pain as the paramedic attempts to move his leg.

EPISODE 5 - PARTY FEARS TWO

MICHELLE:

Sorry about that, but we need to move you onto a gurney and get you into the back of the ambulance.

JIM:

Patrick! Patrick!

Patrick is standing right behind Jim.

PATRICK:

I'm right here.

JIM:

Can you lock up tonight?

PATRICK:

Yes, no worries.

JIM:

The keys are in my desk drawer. You might have to open up in the morning if I can't come in. You know the code for the safe, don't you?

PATRICK:

Yes, it's sixty-eight, twenty...

JIM:

Yes!! Okay, you don't have to shout it out in front of everyone.

Jim winces again as Michelle and her colleague prepare to lift Jim onto the gurney. They place him into the back of the ambulance. Natalie gets in too.

JIM: (CONT'D)
I'm sure it's broken. It's so painful.

Everybody ignores Jim's moans.

MICHELLE:
You going to keep him company?

JIM:
You don't have to, Natalie.

NATALIE:
Of course, I do. You'll want to see a friendly face when you come back from your x-ray.

Michelle shuts the rear doors of the ambulance, gets in the passenger side and the vehicle drives off.

SHOT OF AMBULANCE DRIVING AWAY UP THE ROAD FROM THE SHOP.

FADE TO:

EPISODE 5 - PARTY FEARS TWO

ACT 3, SCENE 4 EXT. HOSPITAL MAIN ENTRANCE 5.20 PM

SHOT OF NATALIE'S PHONE. IT SHOWS 5.20 PM

The ambulance draws up and stops outside the hospital's main entrance. Michelle gets out and opens the rear doors. A porter arrives, pushing a wheelchair.

MICHELLE:
It'll be easier to get you into a wheelchair. There might be a bit of a wait to get into X-ray and it'll be more comfortable for you to be seated.

JIM:
What- even if it's broken?

MICHELLE:
Jim, can you move it at all?

Through cries of anguish, Jim manages to move his foot in a circular motion.

MICHELLE: (CONT'D)
There you are. I doubt very much if you could do that if it was broken.

Michelle and the male paramedic get Jim out of the ambulance and manoeuvre him into the wheelchair. They gently lift his leg onto the leg rest.

MICHELLE: (CONT'D)
Alright, Jim, we'll leave you now in the safe hands of the porter. Good luck. I hope it's not too bad.

Jim is busy trying to suppress his painful moans, so Natalie answers for him.

NATALIE:
Thanks, Michelle.

The porter wheels Jim into the hospital and to the reception.

NATALIE: (CONT'D)
There is one thing good that's come out of this?

JIM:
What 'good' has come out of this? I'm a cripple.

NATALIE:
You've got the perfect excuse not to go to Vanessa's party now.

JIM:
Oh, yes. Yes, you're right. I hadn't thought of that.

Jim attempts a smile, but it quickly disappears as he sees a man on crutches walk towards him. He's with a female companion.

JIM: (CONT'D)
Oh, no.

NATALIE:
What is it?

JIM:
Oh, no. It's him.

EPISODE 5 - PARTY FEARS TWO

NATALIE:
Who's 'him'?

Jim beckons Natalie to come closer. She bends down to listen to Jim who talks to her in her ear.

JIM:
I was driving to work this morning and I accidentally hit my car horn at a zebra crossing. This guy in a wheelchair thought I was trying to hurry him up. I tried to apologise, but he got very haughty and didn't want to know, so... I had a go at him. And that's him, walking toward us.

NATALIE:
Oh, Jim...

JIM:
Please don't recognise me. Please don't recognise me. Please don't recognise me.

The man on crutches does indeed recognise Jim sitting in the wheelchair.

JIM: (CONT'D)
Shit! He's recognised me.

The man does not confront him. He gives Jim the once over, nods and smiles. He speaks to his companion, loudly enough for Jim to hear.

MAN ON CRUTCHES:
You know, God does indeed work in mysterious ways. Karma really is a bitch, isn't it?

He hobbles off and out of the hospital. Jim looks embarrassed and forlorn.

NATALIE:

Jim, sometimes, you have just got to let things go. Most things aren't worth the hassle. It's your ego that's probably more damaged than your ankle, you know?

JIM:

You're probably right. It's nice to have you around as the voice of reason.

Natalie puts her hand on Jim's shoulder. The porter then beckons Jim to follow him.

NATALIE:

Well, I ain't going anywhere. Not yet, anyway. Your bruised ego will recover, as will your twisted ankle. Come on, let's get to X-ray.

Natalie pushes him in the direction of the X-ray department.

SHOT OF NATALIE WHEELING JIM AWAY, FOLLOWING THE PORTER.

END OF ACT 3 AND EPISODE

Episode 6 - True Colours

Written by Elliot Stanton

ACT ONE

ACT 1, SCENE 1. INT. JIM'S CAR. [8.30 AM]

SHOT OF CAR CLOCK. IT SHOWS 8.30 AM.

JIM brakes at the traffic lights. He notices a good-looking woman in the car in the next lane. He picks up his take-away coffee cup. He nods to her and as he does, the plastic top comes off the cup and he spills coffee over him. The woman laughs and the lights turn green. Fortunately, the coffee isn't too hot, so the only thing that hurts Jim is his pride.

JIM:
Unbelievable. Just unbelievable. Look at the state of me.

Jim drives the remaining short distance to work and parks up.

FADE TO:

EPISODE 6 - TRUE COLOURS

ACT 1, SCENE 2. INT. SHOP OFFICE. [8.40 AM]

SHOT OF JIM'S WATCH. IT SHOW'S 3.30. IT HAS STOPPED.

Jim undoes his shirt and wipes down his chest. Then, he frantically rubs his shirt with a damp tea towel, but to little effect.

JIM:
I wouldn't mind so much, but this is a brand new shirt and it wasn't cheap either. I'm bloody cursed, I am - bloody cursed.

There's a knock on the back door. It is NATALIE. She is dressed in tight jeans, black knee-high boots, a jumper with a plunging neckline and a leather bolero jacket.

JIM: (CONT'D)
Hello. You look nice.

NATALIE:
Well, hello there. Is it dress-down Saturday?

JIM:
What?

NATALIE:
You appear to be wearing your shirt, undone almost to the waist. I feel somewhat overdressed for the occasion.

JIM:
Oh, no, I clumsily spilled half a cup of coffee down myself in the car.

NATALIE:
Oh my. Are you alright? You didn't burn yourself, did you?

Natalie looks concerned and checks out Jim's chest for burns.

JIM:

No, it wasn't that hot, fortunately.

NATALIE:

It's lucky that we're not open today, I suppose. The painters *are* still coming in, aren't they?

JIM:

I expect so. At least, I haven't heard anything to the contrary.

Jim's phone beeps. It's a message from the decorators.

JIM: (CONT'D)

And as if by magic…

NATALIE:

The decorator?

JIM:

Yep. 'Won't be there until 11 am. Sorry for the inconvenience. Wojciech.'

NATALIE:

That's not too bad. The last time my parents had the house decorated, they were two days late, not two hours.

JIM:

As long as they're here by 11, and I truly doubt they will. Mind you, they'll have to bear the wrath of Vanessa. This is her gig - she's organised this. I don't care if they turn up at all.

EPISODE 6 - TRUE COLOURS

NATALIE:
But in the meantime, you have a more pressing matter.

JIM:
What?

NATALIE:
That shirt.

JIM:
Oh yes. At least I have a chance to go out and get another one.

NATALIE:
Get a lilac one. I think the colour will suit you. I'm good with colours and matching things together.

JIM:
You think lilac matches me?

NATALIE:
Yep. It'll set off your blue eyes nicely.

JIM:
Do I have blue eyes?

NATALIE:
Yes, Jim. You have blue eyes.

JIM:
I thought they were more green-y

Natalie moves in very close to Jim and stares directly into his eyes. She stares for several seconds.

NATALIE:
Definitely more blue than green, Jim.

JIM:
Well, you'd know. You're good with colours.

Natalie steps back.

NATALIE:
Go on, you'd better get off. You can't walk around with your coffee-stained shirt undone to the waist all day. Well, you can if you want, it's your business.

The spell is broken. Jim clears his throat.

JIM:
I won't be too long. Let Patrick in when he turns up.

NATALIE:
Of course.

Jim leaves the shop by the back door, leaving Natalie at his desk looking through Facebook on her phone. She checks her ex-boyfriend, Kit's status. She reads it out aloud.

NATALIE: (CONT'D)
'Feeling unhappy. I think I've made the biggest mistake of my life and I don't know how to rectify it.'
Blimey, maybe he is genuine, after all.

She agonises for a moment about texting him, but decides not too.

PATRICK knocks on the back door and Natalie lets him in.

EPISODE 6 - TRUE COLOURS

PATRICK:

You look nice.

NATALIE:

Thanks. I'm wearing my civvies as we're not opening today. I see you are too, and some.

Patrick is wearing dirty, ripped jeans and an old and well- worn Metallica tour T-shirt.

PATRICK:

I thought the decorators might want some help, so I didn't want to wear anything I'd get ruined.

NATALIE:

I don't think they'll need your help, Patrick. They're professional decorators. At least, I think they are. They've already contacted Jim to say they'll be late.

PATRICK:

Where *is* Jim, by the way?

NATALIE:

He had to pop out.

PATRICK:

So, how are you keeping?

NATALIE:

Since yesterday? Good, thanks. You?

PATRICK:

Yeah fine. You haven't heard from... from...err...

NATALIE:

Who?

PATRICK:

Kit.

NATALIE:

No. Thankfully not. Not a dicky bird.

Natalie looks down at her phone. Kit's Facebook page is still on her screen. She snatches the phone and closes the app.

There's a knock at the front door. Patrick and Natalie go to see who it is and all they can see outside the shop is a cluster of five-foot-tall pot plants.

PATRICK:

What's going on here?

A man walks into view with another plant. He knocks again. Patrick goes to open the door.

PLANT DELIVERY MAN:

Delivery from Galbraith's Garden Centre - From our nursery to your door.

PATRICK:

Sorry?

PLANT DELIVERY MAN:

Delivery from Galbraith's Garden Centre - From our nursery to your door.

EPISODE 6 - TRUE COLOURS

The delivery man points to the company logo on his red gilet.

PATRICK:

I heard what you said, but this is a pawnbroker's shop, not a tanning salon.

Natalie laughs, heartily.

NATALIE:

That's good - for you.

PATRICK:

Thanks. (He pauses) What do you mean, 'for me'?

PLANT DELIVERY MAN:

Excuse me, but are you going to sign for these?

PATRICK:

They're not for us, mate.

The delivery man holds up the delivery invoice and reads it aloud.

PLANT DELIVERY MAN:

'4 times Yucca Elephantipes, twin stem in pots' to be delivered to... 'Mr James Trueman, Trueman's Pawnbrokers, 42 High Street,' blah, blah, blah. This is Trueman's Pawnbrokers, isn't it?

NATALIE:

It is. I suppose you'd better bring them in. Have they been paid for -as Mr Trueman isn't in?

PLANT DELIVERY MAN:

Yes, all paid for by (CHECKS THE INVOICE)... Mrs Trueman.

NATALIE:

A surprise from Vanessa. I didn't think Jim would be the sort of person to have plants around the place. (TO THE DELIVERY MAN) I suppose you'd better bring them all in.

The delivery man carries them in one at a time and asks Natalie to sign the docket. She does and is handed the bottom copy before the delivery man leaves.

PATRICK:

Jim hates plants.

NATALIE:

What?

PATRICK:

He doesn't see the point in buying flowers or plants as they just die around him.

Once a customer bought him in a potted azalea from her garden. As soon as she handed it to him, you could see the thing physically wilt in front of our eyes. He doesn't trust them.

NATALIE:

He hates and doesn't trust plants and flowers?

PATRICK:

And vegetables.

NATALIE:

Vegetables too?

PATRICK:

Unless they're in a curry, pasty, spring roll... In fact, unless its curried, in pastry, fried or inside something fried, he won't touch them. Oh, and mushy peas. He likes his mushy peas.

EPISODE 6 - TRUE COLOURS

NATALIE:
Thanks for that vital information, Patrick. I'll be sure to remember it.

FADE TO:

ACT1, SCENE 3. INT. OFFICE [9.15 AM]

SHOT OF CLOCK ON OFFICE PHONE DISPLAY. IT SHOWS 9.15 AM.

The backdoor opens and in walks Jim.

JIM:
I had to try three shops, but finally found one. Have a look at this.

Jim takes out a lilac shirt form a plastic bag.

JIM: (CONT'D)
It was the last one they had in my size. I'll pop into the kitchen to… what the hell are they?

Looking over Natalie's shoulder, Jim notices the plants.

PATRICK:
Surprise!!

JIM:
Where on earth did they come from?

NATALIE:
They were just delivered. I take it you didn't know anything about them?

JIM:

No, I hate…

NATALIE:

Plants. Yes, I've heard.

Natalie hands the invoice to Jim.

JIM:

Vanessa. I might have known. How much? A hundred and thirty quid? Why does that woman always have to get involved in my business?

PATRICK:

It's her business as well.

JIM:

Are you trying to wind me up, Patrick? Because, if you are, it's working.

Jim walks into the shop to take a closer look.

JIM: (CONT'D)

Look at them. They're massive. What does she expect me to do with them?
Looking up, he sees a spectre outside the door. It's VANESSA.

PATRICK:

Bloody hell. Right on cue.

Jim unlocks the door to let her in.

VANESSA:

Ah, they've turned up then?

JIM:
I'll take that as a rhetorical question. Whatever were you thinking?

VANESSA:
I thought they'd go with the updated colour scheme.
Here, I've got a couple of things for you. Look at the state of you.

She notices Jim's stained shirt.

VANESSA: (CONT'D)
I seen you've spilt something down your shirt? Some things never change.

An embarrassed Jim zips his jacket up. Out of a bag, Vanessa takes out three small paintings of The Victoria Falls.

VANESSA: (CONT'D)
You can stick them on the wall. Oh, and you remember that little water feature we had in the garden? Well, I had it cleaned up and I thought it would look nice in the corner of the shop. I'll bring it in next week.

JIM:
Are you serious?

VANESSA:
Yes, of course.

JIM:
And how will a forest of Yucca plants, cheap fairground prize pictures of waterfalls and a urine-inducing water feature improve the ambiance of what is, unless you've forgotten, a high street pawnbrokers, and not a dodgy back-street travel agent…from 1967? Hold on a moment; what *updated* colour scheme?

VANESSA:

I texted the decorators to say we'd changed our mind about the colour and wanted a darker shade of green.

JIM:

We changed *our* minds?

Vanessa takes a colour palette out of her bag and points out the colour to Jim.

VANESSA:

Look, it's called 'Enchanted Eden.'

JIM:

'Enchanted Eden?' I think I would call that 'Primordial Sludge.'

VANESSA:

Oh, James, you haven't got a clue, have you? Anyway, it's too late now. By the way, where are they?

JIM:

Wojciech messaged me earlier to say they were delayed and will be here at

11 am. They better be finished by tomorrow as I need to be open by Monday.

VANESSA:

They will be. Penelope had them and said they were very fast and efficient.

JIM:

Well, if Penelope said so, then it must be true.

VANESSA:

Don't be so cynical. She has exquisite taste. Anyway, I must be off as I'm taking Christopher for tea at The Café Royal this afternoon and I need to prepare. These nails won't manicure themselves. I'll call you later to see how they're getting on.

JIM:

I'm sure you will. By the way, who paid for these plants?

VANESSA:

We did, James. We're still business partners, aren't we?

Vanessa leaves the premises, leaving Jim among the unwanted vegetation. A moment later, a familiar voice from outside disturbs Jim's moment of solitude. He looks up to see MRS MULLANEY.

MRS MULLANEY:

Cooey, Jimmy! It's me.

Jim opens the door.

JIM:

Hello, Elaine. How are you?

MRS MULLANEY:

You're shut?

Jim looks around exaggeratedly.

JIM:

Yes, we are. What on earth can be going on?

MRS MULLANEY:
Oh, you're getting the shop decorated?

JIM:
Ah, that must be it, then.

MRS MULLANEY:
In that case, I won't keep you. Here you are, I bought you these. They're mini samosas.

Mrs Mullaney pulls out a Tupperware box out of a shopping bag and hands it to Jim.

MRS MULLANEY: (CONT'D)
Just a word of warning, though - I made them in two batches, only in one batch, I forgot to put any spices in.

JIM:
Oh, that's alright then.

MRS MULLANEY:
And in the other batch, I accidentally put double the required amount.

JIM:
That's not alright. In your cooking, that's quadruple.

MRS MULLANEY:
Oh, Jimmy. Stop teasing. Anyway, silly old me, I put them all together in that box, so they're all mixed up.

JIM:
Don't worry about that, Elaine. I'm sure they'll be absolutely delicious - spicy or not.

EPISODE 6 - TRUE COLOURS

MRS MULLANEY:

You are kind. I'll see you next week then. I can't wait to see the lovely freshly-decorated shop. It's so exciting.

Mrs Mullaney toddles away and Jim shuts and locks the door again.

JIM:

Exciting? Is it? I'm not holding my breath.

Jim looks down at the box of samosas and has an idea. He takes them back into the office.

JIM: (CONT'D)

Right guys, I need three glasses for water; we're playing a game.

PATRICK:

What game?

JIM:

Indian roulette.

NATALIE:

What's Indian roulette?

JIM:

It's a game where you take one of Mrs Mullaney's mini samosas out of the box and eat the whole thing at once. Some are not spiced and some are double spiced. They all look the same, so that's the jeopardy. The last one standing, wins.

NATALIE:

I think I'll pass, thanks, but I'll be happy to observe the carnage.

JIM:

You in, Patrick?

PATRICK:

Yeah, why not?

Jim sits at his desk and Patrick sits opposite him. Jim opens a desk drawer and takes out a red tie, which he ties around his head like a bandana, (a la The Deer Hunter). Natalie brings in two glasses of water.

JIM:

The rules are simple. We take it in turns to eat a samosa, which you have to eat it in one go. The first person to take a drink of water, loses. Alright?

PATRICK:

Let's do it!

Jim flips a coin.

JIM:

Call.

PATRICK:

Heads.

JIM:

It's tails. I win. I elect to go second.

Patrick steadies himself and looks over the box of samosas.

JIM: (CONT'D)

Come on, take one. They all look the same. You'll get no clues.

EPISODE 6 - TRUE COLOURS

Patrick cautiously picks one out. He draws a deep breath and places one in his mouth and begins to chew.

JIM: (CONT'D)
Oooh, has he been lucky and chosen an unspiced one?

Suddenly, Patrick's eyes widen and his face begins to turn red. He coughs and splutters and grabs his glass of water, downing it in one. He then grabs Jim's water and chugs it down. Natalie starts to laugh. Jim follows suit.

JIM: (CONT'D)
That was quick! Oh dear, Patrick, what have you done?

PATRICK:
Bloody hell. How much chilli powder did she put in these?

Patrick rushes into the kitchen with his glass to fill it up again.

JIM:
I win!

NATALIE:
I guess you're just 'Lucky Jim'.

JIM:
Well, I wouldn't go that far.

NATALIE:
No, you'd probably drop the contents of the samosas down your shirt.

JIM:

You think?

NATALIE:

Without a doubt.

JIM:

Oh, the shirt! I haven't changed, have I?

NATALIE:

No, you haven't. I was beginning to think you'd grown fond of the coffee stain and weren't going to bother.

Jim picks up the bag with his new shirt and joins Patrick in the kitchen. Natalie checks that the two men are out of sight and picks up her phone. She texts Kit -*I saw your status. We'll talk later.* She places an 'x' at the end, but deletes it, before sending the message.

END OF ACT ONE

EPISODE 6 - TRUE COLOURS

ACT TWO

ACT 2, SCENE 1. INT. OFFICE. [11.30 AM]

SHOT OF TIME ON OFFICE PHONE. IT SHOWS 11.30.

JIM:
(ON PHONE) Yes, Mrs Khan… Again, please don't worry. Your items are absolutely safe… No, they're not due yet. You'll get a letter if you are overdue, but I'm sure you won't be… Yes, I know you'll be in… That's okay. I'll see you soon. Goodbye, Mrs Khan.
Jeez, That woman.

Wojciech and his assistant are laying down the dust sheets in readiness for their task. Even the plants are covered over.

Jim is watching them, arms folded. Jim joins them.

WOJCIECH:
Before we start, everything has to be just right.

JIM:
You know it all has to be finished by tomorrow, don't you?

WOJCIECH:
Yes. Please not to worry, we will have it all finished. It will look beautiful.

JIM:
Well, I doubt that; not with *Enchanted Eden* all over the walls. The customers will think they're in some kind of swamp.

Wojciech carries on without acknowledging Jim. Jim returns to the

office where Patrick and Natalie are sitting around looking at their mobile phones.

PATRICK:
Jim, why are Natalie and me even here today?

NATALIE:
The thought had crossed my mind too.

JIM:
You know, I don't know. I guess I should have given you the day off.

There's another knock at the door. It's a courier holding a parcel.

JIM: (CONT'D)
This could be the reason why Natalie is here.

NATALIE:
Oh no, not again. That's going to be another gift from Kit, I know it.

Jim goes to the front door, past the decorators who are now preparing the walls for painting. He signs for the parcel and brings it into the office and hands it to Natalie.

JIM:
It's for Miss Reyes.

Natalie opens the parcel.

NATALIE:
Oh wow! A Fendi handbag.

PATRICK:
Will you be sending that back to Kit as well?

Natalie doesn't say anything. She is busy admiring the new bag.

NATALIE:
This is beautiful. I always wanted a Fendi handbag and I love this one.

PATRICK:
Well, will it be going back?

NATALIE:
I can't send it back. I should, but I can't.

Both Patrick and Jim look disappointed. Natalie continues to admire the bag. She has a huge smile on her face.

JIM:
Right, you two, I'm taking you out for an early lunch. There's nothing much to do around here.

PATRICK:
Oh, thanks, Jim.

NATALIE:
Yes, thanks.

PATRICK:
Where are we going?

JIM:
We'll try the pub on the corner. They do some nice grub. Come on, let's go.

Natalie puts her bag in the wrapping and places it under the desk.

PATRICK:

You not bringing it with you?

NATALIE:

No, I don't want to risk it. What if I leave it behind or drop something on it?

PATRICK:

That's not likely to happen, is it?

Natalie thinks for a moment.

NATALIE:

No, I'd best leave it here.

Jim pops his head into the shop.

JIM:

Okay, Wojciech, we're going out for a while. Are you two alright on your own?

WOJCIECH:

No problems, boss. When you come back, you will see progress.

Wojciech's assistant nods in agreement.

JIM:

Yeah, I can't wait. By the way, there's a box of samosas in the office. Help yourselves, but be careful; some of them are quite spicy.

WOJCIECH:

Okay. Thanks.

Jim, Natalie and Patrick leave by the back door.

FADE TO:

ACT 2, SCENE 2. INT. PUB. 12.15 PM

SHOT OF A LARGE SCREEN TELEVISION. SKY SPORTS NEWS IS ON. THE CLOCK ON SCREEN SHOWS 12.15 PM.

Jim, Natalie and Patrick quietly peruse their menus in the sparsely-populated pub, with their drinks in front of them until Patrick takes a sip of his cider and breaks the silence.

PATRICK:

So, Natalie, are you going to get back with him, then?

JIM:

For crying out loud, Patrick, you've got all the subtlety of... of...

NATALIE:

A Weight Watchers leader with Tourette's?

JIM:

Good one.

NATALIE:

I thought so too.

PATRICK:

I thought it was a reasonable question, in the circumstances.

JIM:

Patrick!

NATALIE:

It's alright. I have to say, and you might not understand this after what I've been saying about him, but what has he really done wrong? He's a bit of a man-boy who enjoys spending his time with his friends. I knew that when we met. And he's trying so hard to make amends. I just think that perhaps I've been a little too harsh on him.

JIM:

This doesn't sound like the Natalie we all know.

NATALIE:

I know, I don't recognise it too well, either, but I have been giving it thought and… I'm not saying anything for definite, but I think he may deserve another chance.

JIM:

Well, that's up to you. We won't say anything more on the subject, will we, Patrick?

Patrick remains silent.

EPISODE 6 - TRUE COLOURS

JIM: (CONT'D)

Will we, Patrick?

PATRICK:

No, not another word on the subject will pass my lips. Cross my heart and hope to die. If I mention it again, may I be struck down.

JIM:

Are you done?

PATRICK:

Yes.

JIM:

Good. Let's order.

Jim attracts the eye of the barman. Who spreads his arms and raises his eyebrows.

NATALIE:

I think you have to order at the bar, Jim.

JIM:

Of course. What does everyone want?

NATALIE:

I'll have the grilled sea bass and new potatoes.

PATRICK:

How do you like your grilled sea bass, Natalie?

NATALIE:

Er…grilled.

PATRICK:

I'm going to go for the rump steak and chips. I'd like it 'well-done.'

JIM:

Well done? You Philistine.

PATRICK:

I like my steak 'well-done.' What's wrong with that?

JIM:

What's *right* with it? At least you've chosen something quite bland and not spicy. I don't think your stomach will be able to cope with another bout.
I'll go and order.

Jim orders his food at the bar.

JIM: (CONT'D)

…and I'll have the fish and chips, please.

As Jim pays, he gets a tap on his shoulder. He almost jumps out of his skin. It's one of his most annoying customers - a massive six and a half foot, hairy-faced behemoth, named MR CORNIER.

MR CORNIER:

Oy, why aren't you at work?

JIM:

Hello, Mr Cornier.

MR CORNIER:

You skiving off then?

EPISODE 6 - TRUE COLOURS

JIM:

Oh no, nothing like that. The shop's being decorated, so we've come out for lunch.

Jim points over to Patrick and Natalie.

MR CORNIER:

'Allo, boys and girls!

Patrick and Natalie wave back unenthusiastically.

MR CORNIER: (CONT'D)

This is my local.

JIM:

Oh, I must remember that for future reference.

MR CORNIER:

Yeah, there's not many days when I'm not in here propping up the bar, spending my hard-earned money, eh, landlord?

The barman, who is wiping a pint glass, nods sadly in agreement.

JIM:

You mean spending the money I lend you?

There's a moment's pause and Jim immediately regrets what he said. Then a smile develops on Mr Cornier's face and he plants a hard slap on Jim's back, which makes him jolt forward with force.

MR CORNIER:

Ahhh, you're a funny geezer, Jim. I've always said that, haven't I?

JIM:

I'm a regular comedian, me.

MR CORNIER:

Here, I'll be in to see you next week. I need to renew a contract.

JIM:

You do, it's well overdue.

MR CORNIER:

But I always turn up, don't I?

JIM:

Like a bad penny, Mr Cornier.

Again, there's a silence and again, Jim wishes he hadn't made the comment.

MR CORNIER:

You got me again!

Jim takes a step back, anticipating another spine-shattering wallop to his back.

MR CORNIER: (CONT'D)

I look forward to seeing the new colour scheme.

JIM:

Yeah, you won't recognise the place; if you can thresh your way through the fauna. You'll believe your halfway up the Zambezi.

MR CORNIER:

What? What are you on about? (TO THE BARMAN) What's he on about?

I told you he's a funny geezer, didn't I?

JIM:
It's been enlightening chatting with you, Mr Cornier, but I really must get back to my colleagues now.

MR CORNIER:
That's a pity. You know, you should come in after work one day. We can have a right old session, even though I don't have a clue what you're on about half the time.

JIM:
Sounds like a plan.

MR CORNIER:
Right, I must be off. I'll see you later, if you're still about.

JIM:
(UNDER HIS BREATH). I wouldn't count on it, mate.

Jim backs off and re-joins his staff.

NATALIE:
Who was that?

JIM:
That, Natalie, was Mr Cornier. Don't make eye contact with him - excuse the pun.

NATALIE:
He's a bit of a brute, isn't he?

JIM:
You could say that. I think my aching back could testify to that.

NATALIE:
Is he a regular?

JIM:
Yeah, a regular pain in the posterior. We're lucky it's just past midday. You don't want to see him in the late afternoon. It's not a pretty sight… or sound. Heaven knows what he's like at chucking-out time.

Natalie takes a sip of her gin and tonic and Jim sips his pint of Guinness.

PATRICK:
Oh, Cornier/eye contact. I get it.

JIM:
It's like he has a built-in satellite delay. It's quite pitiful, really.

FADE TO:

ACT 2, SCENE 3. INT. PUB [12.40 PM]

SHOT OF PUB WALL CLOCK. IT SHOWS 12.40, THEN ONE OF JIM'S WATCH. IT STILL SHOWS 3.30.

EPISODE 6 - TRUE COLOURS

The barman delivers three plates of food to Jim's table. Natalie can't take her eyes off Patrick's well-done steak.

NATALIE:
I'd say that was over well-done. It looks completely charred to me.

JIM:
You'd need to send it for molecular testing to find out what it once was.

PATRICK:
I happen to like my steaks well-done. Is that a crime?

JIM:
It is if it's a £5.99 bit of rump from a pub, mate.

Patrick struggles to cut a piece of his steak and then puts it in his mouth.

JIM: (CONT'D)
Wait for the crunch…

Natalie notices a dollop of mushy peas on Jim's plate.

NATALIE:
You like your mushy peas then, Jim?

JIM:
Oh yes, I love my mushy peas. I love all peas; garden peas, (large and petit pois); sugar snaps…I'm not sure if there are there any others.

NATALIE:
Really? I heard you didn't like fresh vegetables.

JIM:
Who told you that? Don't tell me - Patrick?

Patrick doesn't say anything as he is still chewing the same piece of steak.

NATALIE:
Apparently, you don't like flowers or plants, and only vegetables if they're mushy, in pastry, curried, fried or inside something that's fried.

JIM:
It's true that I'm no fan of indoor plants or flowers, I don't see the point. And as for hating vegetables - well, I simply told him once that I couldn't eat them as they might be members of his family. Isn't that right, Patrick?

Patrick is still having a little trouble with his steak.

JIM: (CONT'D)
You still enjoying that piece of meat?

Patrick finally swallows his mouthful.

PATRICK:
Snow peas.

JIM:
What?

PATRICK:
It's another variety of pea. Oh, and marrowfat.

JIM:
We've finished that particular conversation. We're now on to your spreading of misinformation.

NATALIE:

Marrowfat is what mushy peas are made from, so we've already covered that.

JIM:

Great, so it's back to peas then?

PATRICK:

What about black-eyed peas?

JIM:

I can't say I like them much -the vegetable or the band.

No one laughs at Jim's weak joke.

NATALIE:

Aren't black-eyed peas, beans though?

PATRICK:

I don't know, but I do know that peas are legumes.

NATALIE:

As are peanuts.

PATRICK:

And kidney beans.

NATALIE:

So are lentils.

JIM:

Excuse me, but I'm going to leave Gardener's Question Time now. My meal is getting cold. I don't know; it's like a Two Ronnies sketch without a punchline.

The conversation is halted as they all focus on their meals for a few moments. Then Natalie points at the menu.

NATALIE:

I see by the photos they do some nice deserts. The photos look great.

JIM:

My rule of thumb is; if the menu has pictures of food, it can't be much cop. However, pubs don't count. The Crème brûlée looks particularly good.

NATALIE:

I love that. My grandmother used to make a Spanish version called, Crema Catalana.

PATRICK:

What's the difference?

NATALIE:

Catalana is made with milk and thickened with egg yolk, where the brûlée is made with cream.

JIM:

Thank you, Fanny Craddock.

NATALIE:

Who?

JIM:

Rustie Lee?

NATALIE

Who's that?

JIM:

Nigella?

NATALIE:

Ah, yes. I see where you're coming from now.

Suddenly a booming voice sounds from across the pub.

MR CORNIER:

You lot still here?

JIM:

Oh, for heaven's sake.

Mr Cornier walks over to the table. He's standing right behind Jim and addresses Patrick.

MR CORNIER:

Having trouble with your steak, Pat?

PATRICK:

Rick.

MR CORNIER:

Sorry. Having trouble with your steak, Rick?

PATRICK:

No, I mean…

Mr Cornier interrupts.

MR CORNIER:

I walked past your shop just now and had a little peek through the door. Your boys are doing a great job.

JIM:

Really?

MR CORNIER:

Nice colour too.

JIM:

Really??? So, you don't think it's too dark, then?

MR CORNIER:

No, not at all. I hope you're not going to put up your interest rates to pay for it.

JIM:

It's just a paint job, Mr Cornier. I'm not adding a conservatory or beer garden to the premises.

There's a pause. Jim tenses up, expecting a solid blow to his back.

MR CORNIER:

Ahh, you really are a funny geezer. A beer garden would be a great idea. I'd never leave.

Jim rolls his eyes.

MR CORNIER: (CONT'D)

Talking of beer. It's time for another one.

Mr Cornier walks over to the bar.

JIM:

Right, you two, eat up, we're leaving.

PATRICK:

What about dessert?

JIM:

I'll buy you an ice cream.

PATRICK:

But it's winter. It's freezing out.

JIM:

I'll stick it in the microwave for a couple of minutes to warm it up for you then, okay? Just eat up. I'd rather have my sinuses play up with paint fumes in the shop, than risk another conversation with that idiot.

PATRICK:

That's not fair.

JIM:

Not fair? Okay, how about we go to the crepe house next to the post office. Is that fair?

PATRICK:

Crap house?

JIM:

Crepe house.

PATRICK:

Oh yes. Nice one! Very fair.

NATALIE:
Fine by me.

All three start to wolf down their food.

END OF ACT TWO

ACT THREE ACT 3, SCENE 1. EXT. SHOP. 2. PM

SHOT OF THE TOWN HALL CLOCK. IT SHOWS 2 O'CLOCK.

Jim, Patrick and Natalie congregate outside the shop. Jim has the shop keys in his hand.

JIM:
Don't look inside yet. I want a moment to remember what a pleasing colour magnolia was. It was natural, neutral and nondescript, just like young Patrick, here.

NATALIE:

Oh, stop picking on him.

JIM:

I'm sorry, Patrick, but this is a big moment for me.

NATALIE:

It's only a painted wall, Jim. If you hate it that much, you can always get it re-painted.

Jim pauses for a second.

JIM:

You know something, Natalie… you're right. Let's go in.

Jim stands, looking at the far wall in amazement.

WOJCIECH:

Something is wrong, boss?

Jim looks at his colleagues. They wait for Jim to say something.

WOJCIECH: (CONT'D)

It is just the first coat.

JIM:

The colour?

WOJCIECH:

Don't worry, it will look little different when we finish.

JIM:

No, I love it. It's the right colour.

WOJCIECH:

Of course. Like you wanted. Spearmint Green.

JIM:

Yes, just what I wanted. Where's your partner?

WOJCIECH:

He had to go home. Not well after eating some of those triangle things you left. Don't worry, he'll be back tomorrow and we will finish the job.

JIM:

Oh... well, that's alright then.

PATRICK:

What happened to 'Enchanted Eden'?

JIM:

I expect it stayed in the Old Testament. I'm not complaining though.

NATALIE:

He couldn't have got Vanessa's message.

The phone rings and Patrick goes to the office to answer it.

PATRICK:

Jim, it's Vanessa for you.

JIM:

Perfect. I'm going to enjoy this.

Jim walks into the office and puts Vanessa's call on speakerphone for all to hear and sits down behind his desk.

JIM: (CONT'D)
Hello Vanessa. How are you this fine, crisp winter's afternoon?

VANESSA: (O.S.)
You sound happy. What's wrong with you?

JIM:
Nothing is wrong. I'm just happy to be alive. How is your day? Looking forward to your afternoon tea?

VANESSA: (O.S.)
Yes, I am. Actually, who is this? And what have you done with James?

JIM:
Can't you just be happy that I'm happy?

VANESSA:
I am… I think. This is awfully unsettling. Did they turn up?

JIM:
Yes.

VANESSA:
Does it look alright, so far?

JIM:
It looks great.

VANESSA:
See, I told you. I do know what I'm doing, James.

JIM:
You do indeed.

VANESSA:

I'm getting worried. This doesn't sound like you at all.

JIM:

I can assure you it is, Vanessa.

VANESSA:

Right then, my taxi's here and I have to pick up Christopher on the way. I'll be in early next week to see the finished job.

JIM:

I'm sure you'll be impressed.

VANESSA:

I'm sure I will.

JIM:

Bye, Vanessa. Have a lovely, lovely afternoon.

VANESSA:

Goodbye James. You are a strange man.

Jim presses the button to end the call and leans back on his chair.

NATALIE:

Jim, I don't want to burst your bubble, but it's only a paint job.

JIM:

Only a paint job? Perhaps, but this is all her doing. She's made the mistakes; not me. This has nothing to do with me. *She* sent a text that wasn't received and then didn't follow it up. *She* didn't hang around to make sure the painter had the right colour paint and *she* didn't twig that my happiness was due to her impending unhappiness.

NATALIE:
Do you not think that you're just a little bit bitter?

JIM:
I'm a lot bitter, Natalie. That woman broke me. She left me...

NATALIE:
I know - a broken man.

JIM:
Exactly. But, this little victory is so sweet. A small amount of schadenfreude can make one's day all the better. You two can go home now. I'll stay and wait for him to finish up.

PATRICK:
Are you sure?

JIM:
Actually, no, you can stay here.

NATALIE:
Jim?

JIM:
I'm kidding. I'm kidding.

Patrick goes to the kitchen to wash up. Jim takes Natalie aside.

JIM: (CONT'D)
Listen, about the situation with Kit - as I said, I don't want to interfere, but I don't want you to put yourself in a position that you'll regret.

NATALIE:

Thanks, Jim, but I know what I'm doing. If I'm not happy, or I feel like I'm being taken advantage of again, I'll bail out, don't you worry about that.

JIM:

Good. It's just that I care about you and don't want you to get hurt.

NATALIE:

I know you do and I care about you, too. Please don't let the bitterness surrounding you and Vanessa get the better of you. You're worth so much more and deserve better.

Natalie leans over and kisses Jim on the cheek, just as Patrick returns from the kitchen. He doesn't look happy at the sight. Natalie picks up her jacket and opens the back door

NATALIE: (CONT'D)

Right we'll be going then.

JIM:

Haven't you forgotten something?

PATRICK:

(SACASTICALLY) What - another kiss?

Jim stared disparagingly at Patrick.

NATALIE:

Oh, my bag.

Jim hands Natalie's bag to her.

NATALIE: (CONT'D)

See you on Monday.

JIM:

See you then. Goodbye Patrick.

PATRICK:

Yeah, see ya.

Patrick shuts the door behind him. Jim watches Wojciech continue his painting and smiles. Next to Jim is the box of Samosas. Not thinking, he puts his hand in the box, picks one out and places it in his mouth.

JIM:

(with mouth full) Oh no. Oh, bloody hell!

FADE TO:

ACT 3, SCENE 3. INT' JIM'S CAR [5.15 PM]

SHOT OF JIM'S WATCH. IT SAYS 3.30.

Jim looks at his watch.

                                JIM:
Oh, the battery must have run down.

In the distance, Jim spies the golden arches of McDonald's.

                          JIM: (V.O.) (CONT'D)
I know I shouldn't be hungry, but I could murder a Big Mac and fries… and six chicken nuggets…and a small hamburger…and a chocolate milkshake… ooh, and an apple pie.
  Just a little detour to the drive- thru, me thinks.

Jim drives in, makes his drive-thru order, pays and collects his food.

                              JIM: (V.O.)
Ah, the smell; I can't resist it.

Jim parks up in the car park and takes a good slurp of his milkshake. The lid becomes loose.

                                JIM:
No, no, no, that's not going to happen twice in one day.

He presses down the lid and reaches for the big Mac. Carefully, he opens the box and, takes out the burger and slowly moves it towards his open mouth. There's a knock on his window. A startled Jim drops the burger, which falls apart and covers his new lilac shirt.

                            MR CORNIER:
You naughty boy! A pub lunch and now a crafty McDonald's on the way home? And look at the mess you've made.

Jim slips down in his seat, while Mr Cornier stands pointing at him and laughing uncontrollably.

CAMERA PANS OUT.

END OF ACT 3 AND END OF EPISODE

Episode 7 - Lonely This Christmas

Written by Elliot Stanton

EPISODE 7 - LONELY THIS CHRISTMAS

ACT ONE

ACT 1, SCENE 1. INT. JIM'S CAR. [8.30 AM]

SHOT OF CAR CLOCK. IT SHOWS 8.30 AM.

It's Christmas Eve and Jim is driving to work. It's sleeting. He stops at the red traffic lights. 'Mistletoe and Wine' by Cliff Richard is playing on the radio.

JIM:
No, I don't think so, Cliff.

Jim changes the station. (SONG PLAYS) 'Children singing Christian rhyme. With logs on the fire and gifts on the tree...'

JIM: (CONT'D)
What? He's got a bloody monopoly. I wouldn't want your log on my fire, mate.

Jim turns to another station. The last few bars of 'Rock n' Roll Christmas' by Gary Glitter plays out.

JIM: (CONT'D)
Whoops. Someone's going to get their P45 for a Secret Santa.

RADIO DJ:
I'm not sure if I wanted to play that.

JIM:
I'm bloody sure you didn't, mate.

RADIO DJ:
Here's a safer bet; it's Paul McCartney and Wings and they're simply having a wonderful Christmastime; not that Gary Glitter wasn't, but in a completely different way...I hope.

(SONG PLAYS) The moon is up. The Spirits high. The spirit's high. And that's enough...

JIM:
Unbelievable. It's back to hospital radio for you, my boy.

The lights turn to green and Jim drives off. He changes the station again. 'Lonely This Christmas' by Mud is now playing.

EPISODE 7 - LONELY THIS CHRISTMAS

JIM: (V.O.)

That's my Christmas in a nutshell. Lonely. On my own in my flat.

Sitting in front of the box, watching 'The Spy With The Goldeneye'; lunch on a tray on my lap, with a paper hat on me bonce. That reminds me, I haven't got much in. Now, what's in the freezer? I know there's a large chicken and mushroom pie and a toad in the hole. Yeah, that'll do me. Chuck on a couple of potato waffles and some frozen peas, bung on some Bisto and that's me done.

JIM:

And what would sir like to start?

We have a choice of the dented tin of Scotch broth or, if you're feeling daring, that bit of chicken liver pâté that's festering beside the empty jar of mayonnaise in fridge door? Yes, that'll go nicely with that unopened plum and ginger chutney that old Mrs Mullaney gave you last Christmas that you haven't has the guts to open yet.

My my, that sounds absolutely delicious.

And for dessert, may I suggest to sir, a small tin of Happy Shopper mandarin segments or our signature dessert - 'A Trio of Delights' - consisting of an individual Bakewell tart with the cherry missing (sorry about that), an economy choc-ice, freshly chiseled from the back of our very own freezer which are complimented by slightly squished Tunnock's teacake. And to round things off, we invite you to sit back and watch the jewel in the crown of UK Gold's Christmas Day schedule - the 1983 Last of the Summer Wine Christmas Special whilst enjoying a chipped mug of Yorkshire Tea and a crescent of After Eight mints.

I say, you spoil me.

So, that's what I have to look forward to.

Jim stops at the next set of red traffic lights. Across the road, Jim notices a couple with three young children- two of nursery age and one in a stroller. The adults are arguing, two of the children are fighting and the toddler is crying. 'Do They Know It's Christmas' plays on the radio.

JIM: (V.O.)
Still, it could be worse... It was worse - Christmas Day after Christmas Day with Vanessa and her insufferable family. Actually, I'm happier on my own. I can get up when I want, watch what I want and eat what I want, even if it does come down to a choice of the contents, an old dented tin of soup or a dangerously-close to sell-by date pâté.

The woman and children storm off, leaving the man standing with his arms outstretched in despair. In the opposite direction, walks a woman with her miserable husband trudging three steps behind her overladen with shopping bags.

JIM:(V.O.)
You know, I'm definitely better off on my own. To paraphrase the smug, self- righteous Irishman with ridiculous sunglasses - 'Well, tonight thank God it's them, instead of me...

FADE TO:

EPISODE 7 - LONELY THIS CHRISTMAS

ACT 1, SCENE 2. INT SHOP. [8.45 AM]

SHOT OF TOWN HALL CLOCK FACE. IT SHOWS 8.45.

Jim greets PATRICK and NATALIE outside the shop and they enter the premises together. They are all carrying bags with presents; Natalie, an overnight bag. The shop is adorned with Christmas decorations and there's a large Christmas tree near the front door.

NATALIE:
I must say that I'm looking forward to tonight.

PATRICK:
The old annual staff Christmas meal. We're still going to The Star of Bengal, aren't we?

Jim stops in his tracks.

JIM:
Yes, why? Oh, nothing. Good.

PATRICK:
Oh, nothing. It's just that I had an Indian takeaway last night. I had a lamb tikka Dhansak and I'm not sure if my stomach can take another one.

JIM:
Really? In that case, let me give The Ivy a buzz and ask if they've had any last-minute cancellations. Maybe they'll be able to fit us in there.

Patrick looks blank-faced.

PATRICK:
No, no need for that. I'll just have something milder from the menu at

the Indian.

JIM:

Are you sure?

PATRICK:

Yes, I'll be fine. Thanks, though.

Jim looks towards Natalie with an exasperated expression. They walk into the office and put their bags down. Natalie puts the kettle on and Patrick opens the safe. Jim sits at his desk and takes his packet of chocolate digestives out of the drawer. He's about to take on out, but changes his mind.

JIM:

You know, I'm not going to let anything get on top of me today. It's Christmas. Let's get some breakfast in. Anyone fancy a roll from the café? It's on me.

NATALIE:

You're in a good mood.

JIM:

I am. It's Christmas Eve and we're going out tonight. Even Vanessa's presence is not going to annoy me. It would have a few weeks ago… in fact, it did up until last night - that was until a little bird (my daughter) told me that all is not well at Casa Vanessa. Apparently, her boyfriend hasn't been so attentive recently and if there's anything that gets up my ex-wife's nose, it's not being the centre of attention. She's also not happy that Lucy is spending Christmas with her boyfriend's family.

NATALIE:

Vanessa still coming with him tonight, though?

EPISODE 7 - LONELY THIS CHRISTMAS

JIM:

I haven't heard anything to the contrary. So expect a cold front sweeping in from the opposite side of the table.

NATALIE:

And what about you? Where are you doing for Christmas?

JIM:

I'll be at home on my own and I'm more than happy with that.

NATALIE:

Oh, Jim, that's sad.

JIM:

No, it's marvellous! I can't wait. Christmas is usually very stressful for me, but this year, it'll be spectacularly stress-free - quiet and stress-free.

An uninterested Patrick waits until Jim finishes.

PATRICK:

I'll have a bacon and egg roll.

JIM:

Please?

PATRICK:

I said, I'll have a bacon and egg roll.

JIM:

I mean…oh, never mind. And you, Natalie?

NATALIE:

I'll have the same, please.

JIM:
You're welcome, Natalie.

JIM: (CONT'D)
And I'll have a bacon sandwich, I think.

Jim takes a twenty-pound note out of his wallet and presents it to Patrick.

JIM: (CONT'D)
Here you go. Don't be too long.

PATRICK:
Why me?

JIM:
Because Natalie's making the tea and because I asked you.

Patrick takes the money and heads for the back door, mumbling incoherently.

JIM: (CONT'D)
Oh, and get a couple of extra bacon rolls, just in case.

PATRICK:
Just in case of what?

JIM:
Just in case you get lost on the way back and you find yourself starving to death on the freezing streets of Winchmore Hill.

Patrick leaves. Jim leans on the kitchen doorframe as Natalie makes the tea. She brings in three mugs and places them on the desk.

JIM: (CONT'D)

So, Natalie, are you still going to Kit's tomorrow?

NATALIE:

I'm going back to his tonight.

JIM:

You've properly forgiven him, then?

NATALIE:

I know he works long hours, and he has a lot of friends, but he's promised to be more attentive. He's genuinely sorry for how he's treated me.

JIM:

He better be, or he'll have me to answer to. I want you to be happy.

NATALIE:

Thanks, Jim. You're a lot more understanding than my parents. We had a blazing row when I told them I won't be at home this year.

JIM:

I'm guessing that they didn't suggest that you all have Christmas together?

NATALIE:

You'd guess right. They gave me the old, 'it's him or us' ultimatum.

JIM:

That's rather extreme.

NATALIE:

It'll blow over. It always does. My Dad's a fiery Spaniard and my Mum's a fiery… well, she's just fiery. I'm not going to budge on this one, though. You'll meet him tonight at the pub. It's a shame he can't come to the meal first.

JIM:

Working late, again?

NATALIE:

I'm afraid so.

JIM:

It's a shame I have no-one to bring along.

NATALIE:

But you do. You have, Patrick.

JIM:

And that is supposed to make me feel better? No, I mustn't be cruel - not today, anyway. He's not such a bad lad and I know I can be a bit harsh on him, but he's such an easy target.
It's so hard to resist. I hope he likes the present I bought him.

NATALIE:

What did you get him?

JIM:

A book of quotes.

NATALIE:

Haha. I like it. At least he'll know what they're actually supposed to be and who said them. Can we put the radio on? I like Christmas songs.

JIM:

Sure, but didn't you notice my tie?

EPISODE 7 - LONELY THIS CHRISTMAS

NATALIE:
No. Your jacket is still zipped up.

JIM:
Oh yes, it is, isn't it?

Jim takes his jacket off to reveal a dark red shirt with a tie adorned with Christmas paraphernalia. He presses a button on the end. It starts playing *Jingle Bells*. Jim looks very pleased with himself Natalie looks somewhat underwhelmed.

NATALIE:
Oh.

JIM:
What?

NATALIE:
Oh, nothing.

Natalie turns the radio on.

JIM:
Carl, the guy who worked here before you bought it for me a couple of years ago. Most ties will just work for a week or two before the battery dies. I can't believe it still works.

Jim keeps pressing the button to stop the tinny din, but can't turn it off.

Patrick returns with breakfast. The tie is still emitting its tune.

JIM: (CONT'D)
Ah, speak of the devil.

PATRICK:

What's that noise? Oh, you're wearing that stupid tie again.

JIM:

I can't believe it still works.

PATRICK:

I'm sure I'll be thinking the same thing all day long.

They all sit down to enjoy their breakfast. *A Fairytale of New York* **is playing on the radio.**

NATALIE:

I do love this song.

JIM:

It never got to Christmas number one, though.

NATALIE:

What did?

JIM:

Always On My Mind by the Pet Shop Boys.

NATALIE:

That's a shame.

JIM:

Not for the Pet Shop Boys, it wasn't.

NATALIE:

What was your first Christmas Number One?

EPISODE 7 - LONELY THIS CHRISTMAS

JIM:

Mine? It was 'All Alone at Christmas With Me Toad in a Hole on my Lap?' A catchy title.

NATALIE:

What? I mean the first Christmas number one song of your lifetime?

Jim and Natalie laugh, while Patrick obliviously starts wolfing down his second roll.

JIM:

Ernie (The Fastest Milkman In The West) by Benny Hill.

NATALIE:

I've heard of him.

PATRICK:

(WITH MOUTH FULL) Who?

NATALIE:

Benny Hill.

PATRICK:

Who's he?

JIM:

Who's Benny Hill? He was one of the original members of Westlife.

PATRICK:

Oh right. Never liked them.

JIM:

I'm sure they feel the same way about you. Right then, I suppose we'd better open before the great unwashed start banging on the door to be let in.

Jim goes to unlock the front door. Patrick finished his roll and gets to his feet. He points to a spare bacon roll.

PATRICK:
(TO NATALIE) Are you going to eat that?

NATALIE:
No.

PATRICK:
Do you mind if I have it?

NATALIE:
Be my guest.

Patrick picks up the roll and holds it in his teeth before he goes to assist Jim. Natalie clears the crumbs off the desk.

FADE TO:

EPISODE 7 - LONELY THIS CHRISTMAS

ACT1, SCENE 3. INT. SHOP [10.30 AM]

SHOT OF WALL CLOCK. IT SHOWS 10.30.

The shop empties of customers and as soon as it does, two Greek women, walk in. They are talking to each other very loudly in their language. Their voices become louder and angrier. Jim and Patrick are behind the counter.

JIM:

Excuse me!

The women continue their confrontation.

JIM: (CONT'D)

Ladies, excuse me.

They still carry on unaware of Jim.

JIM: (CONT'D)

Ladies. Please…

Once again, they continue shouting, unabated.

PATRICK:

Go on, Jim; sort them out.

JIM:

I'm going to have to. This is ridiculous.

Jim walks around the counter and keeping a safe distance, tries once again to diffuse the situation.

JIM: (CONT'D)
Ladies, I'm going to have to ask you to leave the shop. You can't behave like this.

Then, both women turn towards him and begin to berate him. They have him a sandwich and they angrily point their fingers whilst shouting and screaming at him.

JIM: (CONT'D)
Hey, stop this, will you?

They double-team and start pushing him around. The buffeting sets Jim's musical tie off. Patrick is standing, enjoying the spectacle.

PATRICK:
Doing well, Jim. You tell 'em.

The women stop and start laughing at Jim and his tie. They put their arms around each other and leave the shop, still laughing.

JIM:
What was that about? What did I do? Why does this happen to me?

PATRICK:
I'm not sure, but you certainly have a way with women. They know that you're not a man to be trifled with.

Patrick laughs and disappears into the office, leaving Jim questioning what he'd done.

JIM:
(SHOUTS) I'm still determined not to let anything get me down today,

you know.

END OF ACT ONE

ACT TWO

ACT 2, SCENE 1. INT. SHOP [2.10 PM]

SHOT OF THE TIME ON THE COMPUTER. IT SHOWS 2.10 PM.

On the radio, 'Last Christmas' by wham is playing. Jim, Patrick and Natalie are all in the shop, nibbling on some peanuts and crisps.

JIM:

My last Christmas was pretty horrific. It was just me, Vanessa and Lucy, sitting around a big table with no one talking to each other.

NATALIE:

Weren't you divorced by then?

JIM:
We were, but Vanessa and I decided we should still have Christmas together for the sake of Lucy. Big mistake. It's one thing doing that for a young child, but Lucy was already 17.

NATALIE:
I still think it's sad that you're choosing to be on your own tomorrow.

PATRICK:
He's a big boy. He can make his own decisions.

JIM:
Thanks, Dad

In walks MR HUDSON, a large man in a Santa outfit. He's a little worse for wear. Natalie elects to serve him.

MR HUDSON:
You're new. How much for this, sweetheart. It's been in before. One minute.

Mr Hudson puts his hands down his red Santa pants and roots around.

PATRICK:
(TO JIM) Is he going to get his old chap out?

JIM:
(TO PATRICK) Nothing would surprise me with this bloke.

MR HUDSON:
It's alright, love. I'm wearing trousers underneath. Now, where is that damn thing? Ah, got it.

EPISODE 7 - LONELY THIS CHRISTMAS

Mr Hudson fishes out a gold ID bracelet and drops it into the drawer. Natalie picks it out and weighs it. Jim and Patrick disappear into the office, carrying their snacks.

NATALIE:

Don't you like to wear it?

MR HUDSON:

Nah, not any more. I used to, but it's a bit 'now then, now then', if you catch my drift.

NATALIE:

Oh, I see.

MR HUDSON:

And I'm not like that. Although, funnily enough I do have white hair, bad teeth and have had kids sitting on my lap. I'm raising money for the old folks home, you see.

NATALIE:

I'm glad to hear it.

MR HUDSON:

Yeah, I've been outside Sainsbury's since nine o'clock, flogging crappy presents.

NATALIE:

Yes, that's the true spirit of Christmas, alright.

MR HUDSON:

Well, giving a child a wonderful gift from Santa for a small donation from their parent or guardian. That's the official line.

NATALIE:
Better. It's a really good thing you're doing - raising money for those less fortunate.

MR HUDSON:
My sack is empty now, though.

NATALIE:
Okay, you're veering to the dark side again. Right, I can lend you four hundred pounds.

MR HUDSON:
Four hundred? No, no, no, no, no, no, no, no no.

NATALIE:
Am I in 'The Vicar of Dibley' all of a sudden?

MR HUDSON:
I normally get more than that. I still have to buy Christmas presents for me grandchildren….and it's my round at the pub. No, that won't do. Are you sure you know what you're doing? You've only been here five minutes. Where's your guv'nor gone?

Natalie takes the abuse in her stride and backs off.

NATALIE:
(SHOUTING TOWARDS THE OFFICE) Mr Trueman, are you free?

Jim appears at the doorway.

JIM:
Iiiii'm…available.

EPISODE 7 - LONELY THIS CHRISTMAS

MR HUDSON:

I think your girl has made a mistake.

JIM:

Mr Hudson, firstly, Natalie is not 'my girl' and secondly, I have full confidence in her evaluation skills.

MR HUDSON:

Sorry, love. It's just that I always get more.

JIM:

Let's have a look.

Jim looks up Mr Hudson's records on the computer.

JIM: (CONT'D)

It's been in several times.

MR HUDSON:

Yeah, I know.

JIM:

Three hundred, three hundred, three hundred, three twenty and three fifty. We've never offered you four hundred pounds. Natalie is being very generous. In fact, I don't think I'd offer more than three fifty, myself.

MR HUDSON:

Oh, I'll take four hundred pounds.

JIM:

I don't think so. Maybe you should have thought about that before you were so rude to my staff.

MR HUDSON:
(TO NATALIE) I'm sorry. (TO JIM) I'm sorry. Alright?

JIM:
(TO NATALIE) Do you wish to continue serving this gentleman?

NATALIE:
(TO JIM) Yes, I'm fine with that.

She rubs Jim's arm and types up the contract. Mr Hudson remains quiet, apart from a few subdued belches and begins to rock back and forth.

JIM:
(TO NATALIE). Make it as quick as possible; I think he's about to hurl.

Natalie completes the transaction quickly and gives Mr Hudson his money and contract. He looks increasingly unstable on his feet and Jim elects to help him out of the shop.

JIM: (CONT'D)
Come on, you. Let's get you on your way back to the pub.

MR HUDSON:
Yes, the pub.

But as they stagger off to the door, Mr Hudson accidentally stamps a size 12 boot onto Jim's foot and then falls into him setting off his tie again.

JIM:
Agggghhh! You…..

MR HUDSON:

What do you want to put your foot there for?

JIM:

I thought by keeping it four feet away from you would be far enough, but obviously not. Goodbye and happy Christmas.

Mr Hudson leaves the shop and shuffles away.

JIM: (CONT'D)

Idiot! And a Happy Christmas to you too. Natalie, remind me next time, not to get involved in physically removing people from the shop, please.

NATALIE:

Are you okay?

JIM:

I'll be alright in a few minutes. I'm still not going to let this get me down.

FADE TO:

ACT 2, SCENE 2. INT. SHOP [2.50 PM]

SHOT ON JIM'S WATCH. IT SHOWS 2.50.

Jim and Natalie are behind the counter. Jim is still trying to put pressure on his foot. In walks a regular - It's MRS MULLANEY.

MRS MULLANEY:

Cooey, Jimmy. It's me!

JIM:

Here she is. How's my dear Elaine? Merry Christmas to you!

MRS MULLANEY:

And a very merry Christmas to you. Isn't it exciting?

JIM:

It's always exciting to see you.

MRS MULLANEY:

Oh, you charmer. I mean, isn't Christmas exciting?

JIM:

It's certainly painful, I can tell you that.

Mrs Mullaney doesn't answer. Patrick appears on the scene.

JIM: (CONT'D)

Thanks for helping, Patrick.

PATRICK:

What do you mean? I was in the loo.

JIM:

Aren't you always?

MRS MULLANEY:

Hello, Patrick. Hello Natasha.

EPISODE 7 - LONELY THIS CHRISTMAS

NATALIE:

Natalie.

MRS MULLANEY:

Yes. Now I've made something for you. Something Christmas-y to eat.

JIM:

Don't tell me - Pigs in blanket vindaloo?

MRS MULLANEY:

No.

NATALIE:

Goose biryani?

MRS MULLANEY:

No.

PATRICK:

Christmas pudding?

Jim and Natalie look at Patrick in puzzlement.

PATRICK: (CONT'D)

Er…Christmas pudding madras?

They look at him with even more puzzlement.

MRS MULLANEY:

No. Its a box of Christmas biscuits. Look.

Mrs Mullaney takes a box out of her bag and puts it in the drawer under the counter. Natalie lifts it out and opens it up. The biscuits are in the shape of Christmas trees and bells. Jim looks in and takes a

long sniff.

JIM:
There's no herbs or spice in them.

MRS MULLANEY:
Apart from a pinch of ginger and cinnamon.

JIM:
No garam masala?

MRS MULLANEY:
No.

NATALIE:
No chilli powder?

MRS MULLANEY:
No.

PATRICK:
Er… no catnip?

Jim and Natalie again look at Patrick with puzzlement.

PATRICK: (CONT'D)
Catnip is a herb. Look it up, if you don't believe me.

MRS MULLANEY:
No, nothing like that. Try one.

They all try a biscuit and look at each other in amazement.

EPISODE 7 - LONELY THIS CHRISTMAS

NATALIE:
They're...delicious, Mrs Mullaney.

JIM:
Very tasty, Elaine.

PATRICK:
Definitely no catnip.

Mrs Mullaney looks very proud.

MRS MULLANEY:
Did I tell you my grandson is over from New Zealand?

JIM:
You did, Elaine. That's wonderful for you. You're having Christmas at your daughter's, aren't you?

MRS MULLANEY:
I am. I always do. She's been so good to me. She doesn't want me to lift a finger. I feel a bit guilty really, as I always like to cook something to take around. But she said, 'Mum, after last year, please don't cook anything for me'. She's so thoughtful.

NATALIE:
Why, what happened last year?

MRS MULLANEY:
I insisted on cooking the turkey, but I thought I'd try something a little bit different. The delicate flavours in my Peri-peri turkey made it so filling that no one could finish their plates. So, under duress, I promised to put my feet up this year and let her cook.

JIM:

I think I agree with her. Take it easy and let someone else take the strain.

MRS MULLANEY:

Yes, You're right. I'm not getting any younger and I think my days of cooking are nearing an end.

JIM:

Oh, thank God.

MRS MULLANEY:

Sorry?

JIM:

Thank God that you're going to take a break from that. You're far too good to people, you know, Elaine.

MRS MULLANEY:

Ahh, thank you, Jimmy. But don't worry, I'll still be making the odd lunch for my boys…and Natasha.

NATALIE:

Natalie.

MRS MULLANEY:

Yes.

JIM:

Oh, joy.

MRS MULLANEY:

Anyway, I must be on my way. I have to pick out what to wear tomorrow. You three have a wonderful Christmas, won't you?

EPISODE 7 - LONELY THIS CHRISTMAS

JIM, NATALIE & PATRICK:
We will. Bye.

Mrs Mullaney leaves the shop and the staff fervently dig into their spice-free biscuits.

FADE TO:

ACT 2, SCENE 3. INT. OFFICE [3. PM]

SHOT OF THE TIME ON PATRICK'S PHONE. IT SHOWS 3 PM.

The staff are still enjoying Mrs Mullaney's biscuits with a mug of tea.

JIM:
I guess no one is having lunch today?

NATALIE:
It's three o'clock; we've been stuffing our faces all day and we're got a big meal in a few hours, so I'm going to pass.

PATRICK:
When are we going to open our presents?

JIM:
I clean forgot. Let's do them now. I don't expect we'll get many more customers.

They all pick up their bags and exchange gifts. Patrick opens Jim's gift first.

JIM: (CONT'D)
Now you'll be able to read some great, historical quotes said by brilliant people.

PATRICK:
Some of us think Katie Price and David Beckham are brilliant too, in their way.

JIM:
Then, some of us are wrong. Go on open Natalie's one.

Patricks unwraps a box. Inside is a pair of black-stoned cufflinks

PATRICK:
Thanks, Natalie.

NATALIE:
I thought they'd go well with your... Metallica T-shirt.

PATRICK:
Your turn, Natalie.

Natalie unwraps a Paisley pashmina scarf from Patrick.

NATALIE:
Oh, this is lovely, Patrick. I thought we said we'd keep them to under a fiver? But I love it. Thank you.

Natalie goes to the mirror and tries it on. Jim leans over to Patrick.

EPISODE 7 - LONELY THIS CHRISTMAS

JIM:

One of your sister's?

PATRICK:

Yep. She didn't like it.

JIM:

Thought so.

Natalie tears the paper off Jim's present. It's a Fendi bag tag.

NATALIE:

(GASPS) Oh, Jim…

JIM:

Don't get too excited, it's only a knock-off one. You can't get a real one for a fiver.

NATALIE:

I know, but it's so thoughtful of you. Thank you.

She kisses Jim on the cheek.

PATRICK:

Ahem!

Natalie gives Patrick a kiss too.

NATALIE:

Now for you, Jim.

Jim opens Patrick's gift first. It's a mini Oscar-type statue with the legend - 'World's Best Boss'.

				JIM:
Thanks, Patrick. That's really nice.

				PATRICK:
I couldn't find one with 'Winchmore Hill's Most Adequate Boss' on it.

				JIM:
(SARCASTICALLY) But the sentiment is touching all the same. Thanks. I really appreciate it.

				PATRICK:
Do you?

				JIM:
Yes, I do.

				PATRICK:
That's good, because I was going to ask you for a pay rise.

				JIM:
Oh, go on then.

				PATRICK:
(EXCITEDLY) You're saying yes? I can have a pay rise?

				JIM:
No, I mean 'go on then', you can ask.

				PATRICK:
Can I have a pay rise?

				JIM:
No.

EPISODE 7 - LONELY THIS CHRISTMAS

The front door opens and a group of five teenage children come in, laughing, shouting and jostling one another.

JIM: (CONT'D)

I'm not having that.

Jim gets up and confronts the teenagers.

JIM: (CONT'D)

Come on, guys, this isn't a playground.

CHILD #1:

A playground? We're not seven-year- olds, Grandad.
JIM:
So why are you behaving like seven- year-olds? Come on, out!
ALL THE BOYS:
Ooooooh!!

CHILD #1:

Okay, Grandad. Keep your wig on.

Jim shoos them out the open door, but is nudged into the Christmas tree, which falls on him. Attempting to stop it falling to the ground, Jim jars his knee.

JIM:

Arggghhh!

Jim's tie is pressed into action again. The boys laugh. Natalie comes to Jim's aid.

NATALIE:

You boys should leave now if you know what's good for you.

Patrick makes his presence known and the boys run off, laughing.

NATALIE: (CONT'D)
Are you alright?

JIM:
Yeah, I'll be fine. This is all because I was determined not to get riled today. This place is mocking me. What's the point of trying to be happy when everything is against you?

NATALIE:
Oh, don't say that. It's just an unfortunate coincidence. Take a seat at your desk and I'll make you a nice mug of tea.

Patrick and Natalie follow a hobbling Jim back to the office. Jim sits down and takes his biscuits from his drawer. The tie is still playing. And you can stuff your 'Jingle Bells' too.

JIM:
And this bloody thing is getting on my tits, too.

He rips out the mechanism from the end of the tie. Then, taking off one of his shoes, he smashes it to pieces. Natalie and Patrick look on in amazement.

JIM: (CONT'D)
There, that's better. Calm down, Jim. Calm down. Right, I'm okay now. Just needed to get that out of my system. Right, let's open my last present.

NATALIE:
I'm not sure if you should right now, Jim.

EPISODE 7 - LONELY THIS CHRISTMAS

JIM:

It's fine. I'm calm now.

Natalie tentatively hands over her gift to Jim. He feels the small parcel.

JIM: (CONT'D)

A handkerchief? A very small, thin duvet? A piece of the Turin Shroud?
He rips off the wrapping paper.
Ah, a Christmas tie. *'Jingle bells, Jingle bells; Jingle all the way...'*

Natalie and Patrick stare at the tie and then at Jim. He starts to laugh.

JIM: (CONT'D)

Natalie, I love it.

NATALIE:

No, you hate it.

JIM:

It's from you. I love it. Sorry for being such a pain, guys. We'll have a good night tonight. Chocolate digestive?

Both Natalie and Patrick take a biscuit and laugh at the situation.

END OF ACT TWO

ACT THREE

ACT 3, SCENE 1. INT. INDIAN RESTAURANT. [6.30 PM]

SHOT OF A PICTURE ON THE WALL OF INDIAN DEITIES WITH A WORKING CLOCK IN THE MIDDLE. IT SHOWS 6.30.

At the table, Jim, Patrick, Natalie and VANESSA are seated waiting for the two other guests to show up. Vanessa and Natalie each have a glass of white wine, Patrick, a pint of lager and Jim has a bottle of mixed fruit cider.

JIM:
I have heard that his time-keeping hasn't been quite up to your standards, recently, Vanessa.

Vanessa checks her watch, concerned.

VANESSA:
He'll be here. And where's your fella, Natalie? I'd heard it was all over.

NATALIE:
Then, you heard wrong. I decided to give him another chance. He's coming to the pub, later.

VANESSA:
Just a word to the wise, dear - once you start letting your man off the leash, its awfully difficult to get him back on it again.

JIM:
Now, if I'd said something like that, I'd be accused of misogyny.

EPISODE 7 - LONELY THIS CHRISTMAS

VANESSA:

James, if you'd said something like that, it would suggest that the pink, fruity, cider you have in front of you is not the only thing that's pink and fruity about you.

Natalie and Patrick laugh. Jim gives them both a chastising stare.

JIM:

So, now I can add homophobia to misogyny to your charge sheet. Not that it made sense, anyway.

VANESSA:

Oh, stop it. It was just a joke.

Just then, Natalie's phone beeps. It's a message from Kit.

NATALIE:

I don't believe this. He promised.

JIM:

What's up?

NATALIE:

'I'm so sorry. I can't make it tonight. I've had to stay at my work do. The boss is here and it won't look good if I leave early. I'm sorry. I'll make it up to you, tomorrow'.

(SPEAKING TO THE PHONE) No you won't, mate. You're history.

JIM:

Oh, Natalie, I'm so sorry.

VANESSA:

No one's died, Jim. Natalie, you're better off without him.

323

JIM:

Vanessa, that's not helping.

NATALIE:

Excuse me, I need to go to the ladies.

Natalie leaves the table and walks around the corner to the toilets.

JIM:

You really should learn some tact.

NATALIE:

I'm sorry, but I'm only speaking the truth. He's totally unreliable and he'll only mess her around. It's best she knows now.

JIM:

I'm not going to argue as it's Christmas, but I think your approach is very harsh.

Vanessa looks at her watch.

VANESSA:

(UNDER HER BREATH) Where is he?

JIM:

Maybe he's working late too. Check your phone. You might have a message too.

VANESSA:

Oh, shut up!

Vanessa slides her phone off the table and looks at it under the table. There are no new messages.

EPISODE 7 - LONELY THIS CHRISTMAS

JIM:

If he doesn't turn up soon, we should order.

VANESSA:

He'll be here, alright?

Through the door walks a tall man in his mid-30s, wearing smart jeans, a jumper and a suede jacket with a scarf around his neck.

VANESSA: (CONT'D)

And here he is.

Vanessa stands up and CHRISTOPHER greets her with a kiss on the lips.

VANESSA: (CONT'D)

Jim, Patrick, this is Christopher.

CHRISTOPHER:

Hello Jim and Patrick. I'm sorry I'm late. I was delayed at work.

VANESSA:

Well, you're here now and that's what matters.

Vanessa and Christopher sit down and begin canoodling, much to the disgust of Jim. They are oblivious to everything else.

PATRICK:

Can we order now, Jim?

JIM:

Just wait for Natalie. In fact, I think I'll see if she's alright.

Jim stands up and walks down a corridor to the toilets. He knocks on the door to the Ladies'.

                    JIM: (CONT'D)

Natalie, it's Jim. Are you alright in there?

                    NATALIE: (O.S.)

(SNIFFING) I'm okay. I'm coming out now.

Natalie opens the door. Her cheeks are wet. She's been crying.

                    JIM:

Hey. I know she hasn't an clue how to be tactful, but I think Vanessa is right; he's not worth you getting upset about.

                    NATALIE:

I know that now. I'm not even going to message him back tonight. I'll do it tomorrow and ruin his Christmas.

                    JIM:

That's my girl!

                    NATALIE:

You're very nice to me.

                    JIM:

Why wouldn't I be? You're worth being nice to.

                    NATALIE:

Oh, don't. You'll start me off again.

                    JIM:

Let's go back to the table. Vanessa's toy boy has just turned up. If we're

EPISODE 7 - LONELY THIS CHRISTMAS

lucky, we'll witness a train crash.

NATALIE:
Haha. You are so cruel…but in a good way.

Natalie grabs Jim tightly. The embrace continues for several seconds.

JIM:
(WHISPERS INTO NATALIE'S EAR) Come on, let's go back. I'm hankering for my jalfrezi.

NATALIE:
Half of it you'll no doubt spill down your shirt.

JIM:
Oy, it'll be no more than a quarter. Natalie grabs Jim's hand and they walk back down the corridor. Just then, she whips her hand back and pushes Jim to the side, out of view from the table.

NATALIE:
No. No. That can't be.

JIM:
What? What's wrong now.

NATALIE:
It's Kit.

JIM:
He's turned up? Where?

Jim pokes his head around the corner to have a look. Natalie pulls him back.

NATALIE:

He's sitting next to Vanessa.

JIM:

That's Christopher.

NATALIE:

What?

JIM:

That's Natalie's boyfriend. He just turned up. They're all over each other; it's disgusting.

NATALIE:

Jim, that's Kit. No wonder he's always working late and spent all his time with his mates. Except, he wasn't, he was with her. It's all making sense now.

JIM:

Oh, bloody hell. This is priceless. I can't wait to see her face when he sees you and you let loose.

NATALIE:

Jim!

JIM:

I'm sorry. She's been asking for it, though. And so has he, don't you think?

NATALIE:

I'm not going to say anything.

JIM:

What? What do you mean?

EPISODE 7 - LONELY THIS CHRISTMAS

NATALIE:

I'm going to go back in there and sit down like I don't even know him. I want to watch him squirm. Don't worry, I'll get my own back, and Vanessa will soon realise what a fool she's been too. Just let me play it my way.

Besides, do you really want her crying on the phone to you all day tomorrow, spoiling your day?

JIM:

That's a good point. Come on, let's get back. Are you sure you're okay?

Natalie nods and takes a couple of big breaths and leads the way back to the table. Vanessa and Christopher/Kit are all over each other while Patrick looks very uncomfortable.

JIM: (CONT'D)

Christopher, this is Natalie.

Christopher takes his gaze away from Vanessa and looks at Natalie. He is horrified.

NATALIE:

Hello Christopher. It's a pleasure to meet you.

She holds out her hand and Christopher hesitantly shakes it.

CHRISTOPHER:

Er, hello, Natalie.

Natalie fixes a steely glaze on Christopher.

NATALIE:

Sorry about disappearing. I just needed a moment. My scumbag of a boyfriend has done the dirty on me. I just hope he realises that I can play dirty too.

VANESSA:
As I told you, dear, you need to keep them on a leash. At least I know my Christopher would never let me down.

NATALIE:
(UNDER HER BREATH) Oh, I'm not too sure about that.

PATRICK:
Can we order?

JIM:
Shut up.

CHRISTOPHER:
Excuse me, I've got a phone call. I won't be a minute.

NATALIE:
That's funny, I didn't hear it ring or vibrate.

Christopher stands up and walks to the front of the restaurant with his phone to his ear.

NATALIE: (CONT'D)
I bet he's been called back to work.

VANESSA:
Oh, don't be so silly.

Christopher returns to the table.

CHRISTOPHER:
I'm so sorry, Vanessa. I've been called back to work. There's a problem

with the wiring and it needs to be remedied right away.

Natalie gives a knowing look to Vanessa. Vanessa looks away. Christopher grabs his jacket in readiness to leave.

VANESSA:
They can't call you back this late on Christmas Eve. Tell them you can't go.

CHRISTOPHER:
I can't. I'm sorry. I have to go.

Vanessa tries to kiss him on the lips, but he turns his head and her mouth end up in his hair. He sees Natalie smirking and taking a sip of her wine. Christopher walks out at a pace.

NATALIE:
Patrick, I think we can order now. Waiter!

FADE TO:

ACT 3, SCENE 2 INT. INDIAN RESTAURANT. [7.30 PM]

SHOT OF NATALIE'S PHONE. IT SHOWS 7.30M PM

Natalie's phone buzzes. It's another message from Kit. She ignores it. Everyone else is eating their meals in silence.

PATRICK:
What's wrong with everybody, tonight? It's supposed to be Christmas.

Vanessa takes her phone and goes to the front of the restaurant.

JIM:
(TO NATALIE) Can I tell him.

NATALIE:
Okay.

JIM:
Patrick, putting it succinctly - Kit and Christopher are the same person. Natalie knows it, but Vanessa doesn't. Natalie doesn't want to say anything yet as not to spoil everyone's Christmas. But you don't say a word about this to Vanessa, okay?

PATRICK:
Bloody hell, it's like a scene from..from… something or other.

JIM:
Genius.

EPISODE 7 - LONELY THIS CHRISTMAS

NATALIE:

Just know that I haven't gone soft and Kit or Christopher or whatever he calls himself, will get his comeuppance, in good time.

PATRICK:

Ahhh, Kit is short for Christopher, isn't it?

No one hears him.

NATALIE:

But, you know what they say, don't you?

PATRICK:

There's no fool like an old fool?

NATALIE:

No - Revenge is a dish best served lukewarm . A bit like this lamb korma.

Natalie forks her increasingly unappetising curry.

JIM:

Now, who first said that, Patrick?

PATRICK:

(PAUSES) Scott of the Antarctic?

JIM:

Scott of the Antarctic?

PATRICK:

He went to cold places, didn't he?

> JIM:

Yes, he certainly did, Patrick. He certainly did.

Natalie giggles and this makes Jim smile. Vanessa returns to the table.

> VANESSA:

He's not picking up his phone.

> NATALIE:

Perhaps he's just busy working.

> VANESSA:

Who has to work at 7.30 On Christmas Eve night?

> NATALIE:

I can't think of anyone…apart from your Christopher that is.

Vanessa takes a sip of her wine and sneers at Natalie.

> VANESSA:

So, where's your boyfriend tonight?

> NATALIE:

As I said, he's at his firm's Christmas party up in town and couldn't get out of it.

> VANESSA:

A likely story. He's probably boozing it up with his mates, again, without even a thought for you.

> NATALIE:

Oh, I think I'll be on his mind.

EPISODE 7 - LONELY THIS CHRISTMAS

Natalie's phone beeps again. She doesn't bother looking at it.

NATALIE: (CONT'D)
I reckon he's thinking of me right now.

JIM:
Right then, more drinks?

No one says anything. Vanessa takes her phone to the front of the restaurant again and Patrick goes to the toilet. Only Jim and Natalie remain at the table.

NATALIE:
Thanks for not saying anything.

JIM:
After years of being married to that woman, I know how to keep things to myself.

NATALIE:
I feel quite relieved, actually, but I feel sadder for you.

JIM:
Why?

NATALIE:
I hate to think you being all alone tomorrow.

JIM:
I really will be fine. But what about you? I guess you'll be spending the day with your folks, after all?

NATALIE:
I hadn't thought about that. They'll love that. I won't get a Christmas card from them, instead, it'll be a 'I told you so' card. It'll be the only topic of conversation all day. I can't do that.

JIM:
I know what you mean.

Natalie looks down to her now, cold lamb korma.

JIM: (CONT'D)
Natalie, feel free to say 'no' if you want and I don't want it to sound weird, but, why don't you come to me tomorrow? I've got a family size chicken and mushroom pie in the freezer and I'd struggle to get through it all on my own.

NATALIE:
Have you? A frozen chicken and mushroom pie, eh? That's very enticing. In that case…I accept.

Jim smiles and takes Natalie's hand.

NATALIE: (CONT'D)
All joking aside, that's a lovely gesture, Jim. I'd love to come.

JIM:
Great! One minute, weren't you supposed to be staying at Kit's tonight?

NATALIE:
Oh yes. I've got my overnight back packed in the shop.

JIM:
I may be pushing my luck a bit here, but… Er, maybe it would be easier

EPISODE 7 - LONELY THIS CHRISTMAS

for you…bearing in mind taxis are hugely expensive on Christmas Day… that's even if you can get one…if you'd perhaps…

NATALIE:

I would. There's nothing I'd like more.

Patrick returns from the toilet and Vanessa returns to the table. Natalie takes her hand away from Jim.

JIM:

Obviously, this is just between us.

NATALIE:

Obviously.

VANESSA:

I'm sorry, Jim, but I'm just not in the mood. I'm going to go home. I just don't know what's got into Christopher, but rest assured, I'll find out.

JIM:

I'm sure you will, Vanessa. You always get to the bottom of things.
Jim feels a squeeze to his rump.

JIM: (CONT'D)

Whooaaa!

VANESSA:

What's wrong with you?

JIM:

Nothing. Nothing. Just a twinge. I jarred my knee earlier today.

Jim smirks at Natalie. She winks back.

JIM: (CONT'D)
You know, I'll pay up and we'll all leave.

PATRICK:
Aren't we going to the pub?

JIM:
Nah. Feel free to go yourself. I'm sure you'll go down a storm with our pawn punters, who by now will be out of their nuts.

PATRICK:
Ah, I see your point. I think I'll just head home too.

Jim pays and they all make their way out of the restaurant. It has begun to snow. They walk together in virtual silence the short distance to the shop They halt right outside.

JIM:
(TO NATALIE) Meet me at the back of the shop when the others have gone.

NATALIE:
(TO JIM) Okay.

JIM:
Well then, a very merry Christmas to one and all.

VANESSA:
I doubt it will be.

PATRICK:
And to you Jim; everybody.

NATALIE:
Merry Christmas everybody. See you in a couple of days, Jim.

JIM:
(SOFTLY) Not unless I see you before...

Everyone walks off. Jim goes back to the shop. Natalie re-joins him a moment later.

FADE TO:

ACT 3, SCENE 3. INT. SHOP OFFICE. [8.15 PM]

Shot of Jim's watch. It shows 8.15.

Jim sits on his desk in the dark with Natalie's bag beside him. A street light creates a shadow of someone approaching the door. Natalie enters and walks right up to Jim.

JIM:
Long time, no see.

NATALIE:
I know, but I couldn't stay away from you any longer.

JIM:
Am I *that* irresistible?

NATALIE:
There must be someone who thinks you are..

Jim and Natalie are very close and are looking into each other's eyes.

JIM:

I've got your bag.

NATALIE:

I can see.

JIM:

I'm surprised you can see anything. It's pitch black in here.

NATALIE:

I can see enough.

JIM:

Natalie, I've just realised something - something I should have realised long ago.

NATALIE:

Yes, what's that, Jim?

JIM:

Patrick didn't give me the change from the bacon rolls this morning.

Natalie laughs as the sound of drunk revellers can be heard from outside.

JIM: (CONT'D)

Shall we go then?

NATALIE:

Yeah, let's.

EPISODE 7 - LONELY THIS CHRISTMAS

Natalie turns and exits the shop. Jim sets the alarm and follows her, locking the door behind him. They both get into Jim's car and he drives off. The radio is playing, *Merry Christmas Everyone* by Slade.

JIM:

You've got to love Slade.

NATALIE:

What's Christmas without Slade?

JIM:

Well, it's just not Christmas, at all, is it?

NATALIE:

Jim, I want to thank you once again for letting me stay over.

JIM:

You make it sound like I'm doing a favour for an old mate.

NATALIE:

Aren't you?

JIM:

No. No, I'm not.

NATALIE AND JIM:

Oh no!

Jim changes the station. It's playing The Power of Love by Frankie Goes To Hollywood. Natalie puts her hand on top of Jim's which on the gear shift.

NATALIE:

Jim?

JIM:

Yes?

NATALIE:

Who *did* say 'Revenge is a dish best served cold?'

JIM:

You mean, you don't know?

NATALIE:

No, I really don't.

JIM:

Well, no one really knows for sure, but it was definitely either Ben *or* Jerry.

They laugh together as the song chorus begins.

THE CAR DISAPPEARS DOWN A DESERTED SNOW-LADEN STREET AND OUT OF VIEW.

END OF ACT AND EPISODE.

Contact Elliot Stanton

Tel: 07876 142970

Email: elliotstanton@aol.com

Website: www.elliotstanton.com

The original scripts have been re-formatted for this collection

Printed in Great Britain
by Amazon